carolyn thompson '73

WIDDERSHINS ZOO

TO JEANNE

Zoo Zoo Widdershins Zoo

by
K. B. LAFFAN

FABER AND FABER
London

First published in 1969
by Faber and Faber Limited
24 Russell Square London WC1
Printed in Great Britain by
Latimer Trend & Co Ltd Plymouth
All rights reserved

SBN (paper edition) 571 09273 X

All inquiries regarding professional or amateur performing rights should be addressed to Actac Ltd, 16 Cadogan Lane London SW1

© *1969 by K. B. Laffan*

Zoo Zoo Widdershins Zoo received its first production by the Leicester University theatre group at Vaughan College Theatre on the 23rd November 1968, and was subsequently a double first prize-winner at the National Student Drama Festival in January 1969. The cast was as follows:

MAV	Margot Leicester
BILL	Mick Rodger
RAY	Leslie Perrin
JANET	Anne de Verteuil
MINNIE	Linda Cox
CHRIS	Steve Bould
MIL	Paul Ripppon

Directed by Murray Morison

The first professional production opened at the Nottingham Playhouse on 5th August 1968. The cast was as follows:

MAV	Lynn Redgrave
BILL	Nicky Henson
RAY	Richard Warwick
JANET	Yvonne Antrobus
MINNIE	Sandra Caron
CHRIS	Gordon Waller
MIL	Larry Aubrey

Directed by Frank Dunlop

CHARACTERS IN THE PLAY

BILL
RAY
CHRIS
MILTON
MAV
JANET
MINNIE

MAV *is twenty-one.* BILL *about a year older.* RAY *is nineteen,* CHRIS *eighteen,* JANET *eighteen,* MINNIE *nearly twenty.* MILTON *is twenty.* 'MAV' *is pronounced to rhyme with 'rave'.*

None of the characters belong to any particular sect, movement, philosophy or current fashion. They dress brightly in the modern style with plenty of colour. The men have long hair but not extravagantly so.

The flat in which the action passes is under a boarded roof and it shows in the odd angles of the ceiling. But at one side the roof has been pushed out to provide a wide window which looks down on a street of decaying late Victorian houses. As the street is narrow and on a slope the huge houses across the way can be seen, their plastered fronts blistered and peeling like running sores or botched like scabs, brown and dirty white and russet.

The room is divided in two by a plasterboard wall, the smaller area being the kitchen where there is a gas stove, bath with cover, cupboard and sink. The larger area is the living-room. A stable-type door, the top half of which is permanently fixed back, connects the two. A door leads to the bedroom, another to the landing.

The kitchen is strictly utilitarian. The living-room is bright and gay with plenty of colour. Nothing in the room is new, nor is it particularly well looked after, but none the less it has an air of zest. The upright chairs have been painted with enamel paint, but they do not match, nor do they form part of any particular colour scheme. The settee is maroon, the table oval and in plain unvarnished wood. The curtains on the window are yellow but thin and of poor quality, bought for the colour only. An old brass-bound chest with a curved lid is alongside the door. A couple of white wicker chairs and one dark brown leather study chair complete the seating arrangements. On an old sideboard, half of which has been stripped down to the plain wood, are various clay models and some modelling clay with sticks and wire. The walls have slashes of bright colour here and there. Not pictures, simply colour used as murals. The whole effect is of bright disordered clutter, neither clean nor dirty. There is no plan, no scheme—everything is impulsive but somehow it comes together.

ACT ONE

A living-room and kitchen. The living-room has a dining table and chairs. It is a jumble of old furniture, books, magazines, clothes, etc. The kitchen is entered through a "stable door" and has a stove (gas) and a bath covered by a board. There's a cupboard on the wall for food, etc.

When the curtain rises the stage is empty and although it is morning the curtains are closed, but they let in a deal of gloomy light. Enough to see the door up R. open and MAV *entering.*

She wears a thin wrap. She goes into the kitchen and lights the gas —the kitchen is illuminated only by a small frosted window. This done she goes into the living-room, opens the curtains and searches round the room. Eventually she finds a cigarette packet with several inside, under the cushion of the armchair. She takes one and returns to the kitchen where she lights it at the gas stove. Sits on a stool smoking and waiting for the kettle to boil.

CHRIS *comes in at up* R. *He is thin and twenty. He searches about for a cigarette. He wears trousers, vest and socks.*

MAV (*seeing him over the stable door*): They're on the sideboard.
CHRIS (*turning*): You're an early bird.
MAV: I always have been.

(CHRIS *gets cigarette and lights it.*)

CHRIS: It was cold in there last night.
MAV: We had the overcoat.

(CHRIS *goes into the kitchen and in between puffs at his cigarette he washes at the sink.*)

CHRIS: I've never had an overcoat. I had a mac once, but never an overcoat.
MAV: You get your turn with it.
CHRIS: I know. (*He dries his face.*) I was just thinking that's all.

MAV: What about?

CHRIS: Just how things happen.

MAV: You got any unemployment to come?

CHRIS: You must be joking. I've been out of benefit a month.

(The kettle boils. MAV *makes the tea.* CHRIS *finishes with the towel and goes off. As he reaches the door* MINNIE *enters. She is wrapped in a coat and her bare feet and legs show beneath.)*

MINNIE *(to* CHRIS*)*: You're a right herb leaving me . . . I might have froze.

CHRIS: I had. That's why I got up.

(He goes off. MINNIE *hops across to the kitchen.)*

MINNIE: Brrr. Blimey. *(She shivers, jumps up and down on her toes, rubs hands.)* It's parky when the passion wears off.

MAV: This is all the tea we've got.

MINNIE: I got a quarter yesterday.

MAV: We drink a lot this weather.

MINNIE: "Old Shrinkie'll" get suspicious if I go hanging about there much more. Ooh's lovely!

(She takes a cup of tea and huddles up in an armchair. MAV *also takes a cup of tea and sits.)*

MAV: You'd be better off doing one of the big places.

MINNIE: Little 'uns are best . . . in the big 'uns they're watching all the time. They got mirrors and TV and all that lark. Little places can't afford 'em. *(She cuddles the cup in her hands.)* Any cigs?

*(*MAV *tosses cigs to* MINNIE. CHRIS *comes back putting on his tie, his shirt buttoned but not tucked in. He switches on the electric fire.)*

MAV: It went out last night, remember?

CHRIS: I'll give Ray a nudge. *(He turns to go.)*

MAV: He's got nothing.

CHRIS: He had a florin last night. I saw it.

MAV: That's his emergency one.

MINNIE: The way my blood feels the emergency's here. I've got icicles for corpuscles.

*(*BILL *enters. He is dressed in trousers and a thick sweater.)*

BILL: Where's the tea?

MAV: Go easy—it's all we've got.

(*In the kitchen* BILL *gets a large mug from the cupboard.*
MINNIE *gets up and goes to the kitchen as he turns to the pot with it.*)

MINNIE: Ah ha . . . fair shares. (*She takes the mug from him.*)

BILL: It is fair. I don't have seconds.

MINNIE: If you fill that the others won't even have firsts. (*Hands him a cup and returns to the living-room carrying the mug.*)

BILL (*leaning over the stable door*): Mean old cow!

MINNIE (*pleasantly*): Fat old pig!

(BILL *pours tea.*)

BILL: Golden glittering orbs to you.

MINNIE: And marshmallows to you friend. Squashy ones.

MAV: How do you two get on in bed?

(CHRIS *gets tea.*)

BILL (*coming in with tea*): I get earache, don't you, Chris?

MINNIE: Chris is a gentleman.

BILL: Ooh la did dah! (*To* CHRIS.) What do you do? Bow and ask if you can have the pleasure?

CHRIS: Is there any sugar?

MAV: It's in that.

(BILL *passes the "dredger" of sugar.*)

CHRIS: Oh . . . thanks.

BILL: Well. . . . (*He looks round.*) It's a great life if you don't weaken.

MINNIE: It's a better one if you get a fire going.

BILL: Do I burn the chairs?

CHRIS: I've got a rupee . . . it might fit.

BILL (*taking it*): It might indeed. (*Goes to the meter by the fire.*) The man won't like it, but we've nothing to lose but the shivers.

(BILL *bends to put the coin in the meter.*)

MAV: Something's got to be done.

MINNIE: It'll have to be the old Nat. Assis.

MAV: They won't wear us again.

BILL: It's a bit too big.

CHRIS: Let's see.

MINNIE: They have to cough up. It'd be a disgrace to the State if we froze to death.

BILL (*pontificating*): You are young. You are able-bodied. You can work. England is still a land of opportunity if you have elbow grease and the will to win through.

MINNIE: The Mirror'd give 'em hell I bet.

MAV: Who?

MINNIE: The bloody Assistance people for letting us freeze.

CHRIS: We haven't got a file, have we?

BILL: We've got one a foot thick with the Assistance.

CHRIS: Anything rough 'ud do. It only wants a bit off.

BILL: Get Minnie to lick it.

MINNIE: I'll remember that tonight.

MAV: I thought you were with Ray.

MINNIE: Nuts!

CHRIS (*who has been looking round*): I know . . . doorstep.
(CHRIS *goes out door* C.)

MINNIE: Shut the door, Chris.
(*He doesn't hear.* MINNIE *lifts her foot and prods* BILL.)
Go on, Billie . . . we haven't your fatty protection. We notice draughts.

BILL (*shutting the door*): Ray'll have to split his florin.

MINNIE: He's having a long sleep in, isn't he?

MAV: What's there to get up for?

MINNIE: The tea'll be cold for one thing. (*Goes to refill her cup.*)

BILL: He's always late . . . haven't you noticed? (*Sees* MINNIE *pouring a second cup of tea.*) Here . . . who's on fair shares now?

MINNIE: There's enough for another half cup each.

BILL: Then fill this up!
(BILL *puts his mug in front of* MINNIE.)

MAV: You can take one to Janet.

BILL: She moved in with Ray—she can't expect tea and the overcoat.
(RAY *comes in, a blanket round his shoulders.*)
Greetings Lord and Master. Tea is served!

RAY: What a filthy stinking sod of a morning.

MAV: You might feel better with your socks on.

RAY: With fitted carpets, central heating and double glazing I wouldn't need any socks.

BILL: You wouldn't need any blood either.
MINNIE: Mine congealed in the night.
RAY (*looking at tea in the cup*): Is this it?
MINNIE: It's all there is. Take it or leave it.
RAY (*putting down the cup*): I live graciously or not at all.
MAV: Then you'll have to break into your florin to survive.
   (CHRIS *comes in.*)
CHRIS: I think I've done it!
   (*He goes to the meter. Stops on seeing* RAY.)
   Oh, you're up.
RAY: I was not dead, just sleeping. Surprised?
BILL: Disgusted.
   (RAY *turns and looks at him.*)
RAY: You say something?
BILL: It was just the wind round my heart.
CHRIS: It's still too big.
   (*He goes out again.*)
RAY: What's he up to?
MINNIE: He's trying to get the fire going.
RAY: Well Christ knows we need it.
MAV: It really looks as if one of us will have to get a job.
   (*Pause.* BILL *and* RAY *exchange glances.*)
BILL: Is she guilty of sacrilege, heresy or blasphemy?
MAV: Common sense. We've got to eat.
BILL: That's true. But I don't like the implication that one has to work to do it.
MAV: I don't see any other way, the cupboard's bare.
MINNIE: I'm bloody cold.
BILL: Take a run round the block.
MINNIE: I'd never make it.
MAV: It need only be a part-time job till we get things sorted out.
RAY: What things?
MAV (*about* BILL): He might sell something.
BILL: I have two A levels and a proletarian background. Any offers?
RAY: We'll have to organize a lifting party.
MAV: Where will we lift?

RAY: Usual places.
MAV: It's getting too risky. Ask Minnie.
MINNIE: They're getting to know us . . . even "Old Shrinkie" watches me like a hawk.
BILL: He's been breathing down my neck too.
(CHRIS *comes in, goes to the meter and inserts the coin.*)
RAY: So what? We forage farther afield.
CHRIS: Bingo!
(*A glow starts to rise on the electric fire.*)
MINNIE: Isn't he a bloody wonder? (*She runs over and squats by the fire.*)
BILL: Fair shares! (*He pushes her aside.*)
MINNIE (*pushing*): You've got fat to keep you warm.
CHRIS: Wait a sec.
(CHRIS *lifts the fire away from the fireplace and faces it upstage at down* R.C.)
We can all get round this way.
MINNIE: He's a genius you know. (*Roasts her toes.*) Ooooo . . . 'swonderful.
BILL (*to* RAY): Can you smell roast pork?
MINNIE: Delicious.
RAY: We'll have to do a job, that's all.
MAV: Ah no . . . I'm not having that. A bit of lifting's one thing but proper stealing——
RAY: What's improper stealing?
MAV: You know what I mean.
BILL: It's a matter of conviction!
MAV: Very funny.
BILL: It's true. Pinch a packet of tea, plead sick and you might get away with it. Pinch a pound note and you haven't a hope in hell.
MINNIE: So what does that prove?
BILL: Search me. But he (RAY) could have lifted that Yank's wallet last night but he didn't. (*To* RAY.) Did you?
RAY: I felt sorry for the poor sod.
MAV: I don't like that word.
RAY: What's wrong with it?
MAV: I just don't like it.

RAY: What's a sod but a bit of dirt with grass growing out of it?
MINNIE: There was grass growing out of him all right. Talk about simple.
RAY: That's what I mean.
BILL: Sod as a vulgarism has nothing to do with grass in ears or anywhere else. It's short for Sodomite.
MINNIE: And good night professor.
BILL: Any little thing you want to know—just ask.
MINNIE: Right . . . what's for breakfast?
   (*Pause. They look at each other.*)
BILL: Um . . . I put that to the house.
MAV: There's a tin of beans.
   (*Pause.*)
MINNIE: Large or small?
   (MAV *goes to the kitchen, returns with a tin of beans and a few slices of bread still in the wrapper. She puts them on the table. Holds up the tin.*)
MAV: Small I think. (*Bread.*) Five slices.
RAY: Between six of us. How do we share that out?
BILL: Jesus Christ would have no difficulty.
MINNIE: He doesn't happen to live here.
CHRIS: What about his florin?
RAY: What about your box?
BILL: There's nothing in there.
RAY: That's a tale. (*Kicks it.*) Never sounds empty.
BILL: It's my old suit—deadens the sound.
CHRIS: We could flog that maybe.
BILL: All right—help yourself. Go on.
RAY: We want the key.
BILL: You know there's no key.
MINNIE: You need an elephant to get in there without one.
CHRIS: There's that cupboard in the bedroom too.
BILL: We got my grandmother locked in there. (*To* MAV.) Or was it the landlord's we did in?
MAV: I wish you'd all be serious for a minute.
RAY: If it's share and share alike we've a right to know what's locked away.
MAV: It's never been open that I know of.

RAY: Who locks a cupboard for nothing?
BILL: Exactly. I thought I could smell a decaying corpse there one night—but it turned out to be his feet. (RAY.)
RAY: We could burst it open.
BILL: And if it turns out to be just a way to the roof who stops the draught?
MINNIE: He's right, it's draughty enough the way that window is.
CHRIS: It wants a thicker bit of cardboard.
RAY: We can do this anyroad. (*To* CHRIS.) Gimme a lift.
MAV (*getting between* CHRIS *and box*): Don't start that again.
RAY: What again?
MAV: Banging that about.
BILL (*putting foot on box*): She can't stand the noise.
MINNIE: Nor me neither. (*To* RAY.) Cough up that florin . . . it's quieter.
BILL: And more negotiable.
RAY: I've always had that florin, and——
CHRIS: Well, now's the time for change——
RAY: Not on your nelly, Kelly. We've got to be really on the floor before I touch that.
MAV: If we're not on the floor now where are we?
RAY: There might be something in the post.
MAV: What?
RAY: You did that crossword last week.
CHRIS: And he (BILL) wrote a letter to *Woman's Own*.
BILL: That was to ask advice about me acne.
CHRIS: I can't face beans. (*Getting up.*) I need bacon and eggs. (CHRIS *goes out.*)
BILL: Oh very decisive!
RAY: A bloody lot of good that does if your pocket's empty.
MAV: I suppose Janet's getting up?
RAY: She was flat out when I left her. Why?
MAV: We've got to decide what to do.
MINNIE: We can't all wait on her. Cook 'em and chuck me a bit of bread.
MAV: I mean long term.
BILL: Long term we'll all be dead. Keynes.

MAV (*irritated*): All right . . . sort it out yourselves. (*Picks up tea and a slice of bread. Sits.*)
RAY: Now you've given her the hump.
MINNIE (*to* MAV): Are you having a whole slice?
BILL: You're hogging the fire, let her hog the bread. (*Starts to open the beans.*)
RAY: Don't all start getting bitchy—we've had hard times before.
BILL (*poetically and solemnly*): And we shall have hard times again.
RAY: It's just a question of getting an idea for roping in a few quid.
MAV: We know your ideas . . . rob the Bank of England.
RAY: I wish to Gawd I could——
BILL: It would just about cover the rent we owe.
MAV: Has he been around again?
BILL: Don't fret, he eats from my hand.
MINNIE: Urh!
BILL: I speak figuratively, ignoramus. Not that crowned heads couldn't mess from my metacarpuses without worry. Are we having these hot or cold?
(*He holds up the tin of beans. There is a knock at the door as he does so. Pause.*)
The bums?
MINNIE (*shouts*): Come in!
(*The door opens and* MILTON CHASE *is revealed. He is a young American.*)
MIL (*not quite at ease*): Hi!
(*All turn and look. Pause.*)
MINNIE: Shut the door for Christ's sake.
MIL (*shuts door*): Janet home? (*Pause.*) She fixed for me to call.
BILL: Isn't it our young grass-growing American cousin?
RAY: How's your wallet?
MIL: Yeh . . . I was a fool about that I guess.
(*Pause.*)
I got the right place, haven't I? I mean Janet does live here?
MINNIE: She's still in bed.
MIL: Oh. . . . (*Looks at watch.*) Maybe I mistook the time——

RAY: I'll go and wake her.
MIL: Oh please don't——
RAY: No bother . . . it'll be a pleasure to disturb the lazy bit!
(RAY *goes off. Pause.*)
MAV: You'd better make yourself at home. She'll be hours.
BILL: Show him a woman in bed and he'll usually join her.
(*Pause.*)
MIL: I never realized you all lived together.
BILL: We never realized you'd made a hit with Janet.
MIL: I wouldn't call it a hit . . . I guess she felt sorry for me. Stranger in an alien land, sort of thing.
MINNIE: You warm enough?
MIL: Oh . . . yeah . . . I'm fine.
MAV: We can offer you a cup of luke-warm tea.
BILL: Or some beans . . . they might break the ice. Make you feel at home.
MIL: One thing I hate it's beans.
BILL: You amaze me . . . I thought Americans lived on pork'n beans.
MIL: That's just those westerns.
BILL: You're not a Westerner?
MIL: I'm from Utica . . . New York State.
BILL: That's west of New York, isn't it?
MIL: Well, yeah . . . I guess it is a bit.
BILL: Then you're a Westerner.
MIL: Well you see . . . in America——
MAV: Take no notice of Bill . . . he's always trying to be smart.
MINNIE: And he's always failing.
BILL (*to* MIL): The trouble with the modern Englishman . . . English women! Look at them . . . the mothers of our children.
MINNIE: Not if I can help it.
(RAY *comes in. Goes to* MIL.)
RAY (*politely*): Janet will not keep you long. She's dressing.
MIL: Thanks.
RAY: In the meantime could you lend her a couple of quid?
MIL: Beg your pardon?
RAY: I beg yours. Pounds. Britisher greenbacks.

MIL: Oh you mean money?
RAY: Exactly. She's temporarily embarrassed . . . if it's no trouble.
MIL: Oh, she's welcome. (*Takes out a loaded wallet.*) What do you call them?
RAY: Quid's . . . slang . . . like bucks for dollars. Get it?
MIL: Sure. (*Carefully extracts two notes.*) Two quids.
RAY: Quid.
MIL: Oh . . . just one? (*Starts to take one away.*)
RAY: Two. . . . (*Grabs both notes.*) Quid is plural and singular.
MIL: I get it.
RAY (*with great courtesy*): Thank you.
MIL: You're welcome.
RAY (*to the others*): Look after . . . er . . .? (*Looks inquiringly at* MIL.) We weren't introduced last night. Ray Carpenter. (*Hand out.*)
MIL (*shaking hands*): Glad to know you . . . Milton Chase.
BILL: Of Utica, New York State. Just west of New York City.
MIL: He's great. There's not many folk in the States know where Utica is. It's not much of a place.
RAY: Bill is very knowledgeable . . . and believes in letting people know it.
(*As* BILL *opens his mouth to reply*, RAY *holds the notes before his face and grins.*)
Breakfast is on its way. Make Milton feel at home.
(RAY *goes out.*)
MINNIE: I'd better get some rags on my back.
(*She stands up and stretches, the coat rises and reveals her thighs.* MIL *eyes them.* BILL *goes into the kitchen and heats the beans.* MAV *begins to clear the cups etc.* MINNIE *catches* MIL *looking at her thighs.*)
MIL: Er . . . sorry.
MINNIE (*coolly*): Get used to it. There'll be just as much showing later.
(MINNIE *goes off.* MAV *comes to beside* MIL *to pick up* MINNIE'*s cup.*)
MAV: What are you doing here out here?
MIL: You make it sound like it's way out deserted.

MAV: Most of you Americans stay up in London.

MIL: Guess I'm the one that got away.

MAV: Brum's no place anyone wants to get away to.

BILL (*over the stable door from kitchen*): You want any of these beans?

MAV: Don't make me sick.

BILL: I'll have the lot then.

MAV (*to* MILTON): Some men'll eat anything.

BILL: Waste not want not. They're starving in China.

MAV (*taking cups into kitchen*): Then take them there . . . do you good.

BILL: And offend our American friends. Never! (*In exaggerated Americanese to* MILTON.) I want you to know Mr. President that we stand four square with you in believing that the way to China's stomach is via Vietnam! Kick her there and she's cured for keeps. So are you.

MAV (*coming to* BILL *with saucepan*): You're supposed to simmer these not boil them!

BILL: Don't teach your grandmother——

MAV: It'll ruin the taste.

BILL (*taking saucepan*): I want it ruined.

MAV: But they'll burn.

BILL: Carbon is good for the digestion. It purifies the system, cleans the blood, tones the kidneys, clarifies the liver and plays hell with constipation.

MAV: Your inside must be hell.

BILL: If Dante could see it he'd be in ecstasy!
(BILL *empties the beans on to a plate.*)
Delicious! (*Crosses to table with plate etc.*) How the poor live! (*He attacks the beans with gusto.*)

MIL: I'd have thought you could hold down a good position.

BILL: If you're an agent for the brain drain you are wasting your time. (*He eats.*) I won't say England needs me, but I don't need America.

MIL (*smiling*): I guess America's relieved to know that.
(BILL *looks at him.* MIL *looks away. Pause.*)

BILL (*eats*): You on holiday?

MIL: No. I'm in England to get out of being drafted.
(*Pause.* BILL *eyes him then eats. Stops.*)
BILL: To Vietnam?
(MIL *nods.*)
Cowardice, conscience or convenience?
MIL: I wouldn't know.
MAV (*who has been listening over the stable door*): Mind your own business, Bill.
BILL: I'm interested.
MIL: I'm not ashamed of it.
MAV: I should hope not. Any man who wants war wants locking up.
(*The door opens and* CHRIS *comes in with a load of groceries.*)
CHRIS (*bringing them to the table*): Get the stove going—I'm famished.
BILL: Where the hell did you get that lot?
CHRIS: Telephone kiosk by the car park.
MAV (*moving in*): You bust it open?
CHRIS (*opening parcels*): Had my eye on it for a long time. Easy. And I timed it right. About due for emptying.
(*He puts his hand into his pocket and lets a small pile of coins run on to the table.*)
Keep us going for a day or two.
BILL: They have warning whatnots in those kiosks you know. Touch the till and it wakes the sleeping police.
CHRIS: Well, it had an off day today, didn't it? (*About* MIL.) What brings him here?
BILL: He doesn't fancy holidaying in Saigon.
CHRIS (*handing eggs and bacon to* MAV): Two of each, please. Fried. Bacon crisp, eggs turned. (*To* MILTON.) What's Brum got that Saigon hasn't?
MIL: Peace.
MAV: Any more orders?
BILL: Same for me.
MAV: After that?
BILL: It should make for an elegant sufficiency.
MAV: It should make for fatty degeneration of the heart too.
(*She goes to the kitchen and starts cooking.*)

CHRIS (*to* MIL): You getting out of the call-up?
BILL: That's English for draft.
MIL: Say, you stole that money?
BILL: We call it redistributing the nation's wealth.
MIL: Among yourselves?
CHRIS: Not completely. I intend to send a five-shilling P.O. to Oxfam and save a child.
MIL: To put your conscience right you mean?
CHRIS: I don't have one of those. (*Puts cigarette to mouth.*) Got a light?
(MIL *produces lighter. Lights* CHRIS's *cigarette.*)
BILL: We are not given to the old-fashioned concept of soul searching. We do not intend to perish in a moral Aberfan.
MAV (*calling from kitchen*): Do you want tea or coffee?
BILL: Tea.
CHRIS: Coffee.
MAV: You're not having both.
(CHRIS *and* BILL *look at each other.*)
BILL: Coffee!
CHRIS: Tea!
(*Pause.*)
BILL (*to* MIL): You see nothing's easy . . . not even self-sacrifice.
MIL: I wouldn't say no to a coffee.
(BILL *looks at* CHRIS.)
CHRIS: Coffee it is. (*To* MAV.) Three coffees.
MAV: Does he want to eat?
(CHRIS *and* BILL *look at* MIL.)
MIL: Just a coffee. Oh hi Janet.
(MIL *gets to his feet as* JANET *enters. She is dressed in a mini skirt. Her hair is short.*)
JANET: Any coffee?
BILL: By the grace of Chris's nerve and the Postmaster General's inefficiency . . . yes. (*Calls to* MAV.) Four coffees.
JANET (*to* MIL): I always feel like death in the morning.
BILL: You shouldn't sleep with your mouth open.
JANET (*indignantly*): I don't.
BILL: I have turned over many a night and admired your fillings.

JANET: Beast! (*She throws the cosy at him. He ducks and it flies into the kitchen as* MAV *comes out with plates of food.*)
MAV: Oy . . . watch it. (*She ducks.*)
CHRIS (*taking a plate from* MAV): I'm ready for that.
BILL (*to* MIL): Too many sweets when she was young. Weak parents.
MAV (*to* BILL): You can talk. (*Puts food before him.*)
CHRIS: Where's the bloody sauce?
MAV: If you want it find it.
BILL: My parents were martinets. (*He attacks his food.*) They believed the only way to enjoy life was to do without. I was a deprived child.
MAV: And now you're a depraved man!
BILL (*stopping with food half-way to his mouth*): Happily my depravity is tempered with suavity . . . the mark of the civilized man.
(CHRIS *comes back with the sauce.*)
Thank you.
CHRIS (*snatching it back*): Don't be bloody saucey.
BILL (*to all*): He's swearing a lot lately . . . and witty with it!
JANET: I thought you hated civilized men.
(MAV *returns with the coffee.*)
BILL: True I do. I hate myself.
MAV: That's a laugh.
BILL: Then enjoy it love . . . they are few and far between in this vale of tears.
MAV (*to* JANET): Do you want anything to eat before he gorges it all?
BILL (*to* MIL): She's getting at me.
JANET: Just coffee.
BILL (*takes sauce from* CHRIS): Hey! You use cette sauce to add piquancy to the dish—not to saturate your salivaries.
CHRIS: If you hate yourself I'd like to see you in love!
BILL: Eh?
CHRIS: I'd like to see you in love.
BILL: Ah well watch me with our Janet. (BILL *dives at* JANET *who is in the armchair.*)
JANET: Not this morning thank you. Any cigs? I'm exhausted.

MIL: Here. (*Produces a packet.*)
BILL: Sit down.
JANET: What do you mean I——
BILL: Not you . . . him . . . our refugee from American imperialist aggression.
JANET: He's nice . . . I like him. (*She crosses and sits by* MIL *on the settee.*)
BILL: That's why she asked him here! You wanted a nice man for a change.
JANET: Well, it will be a change, won't it?
BILL: At heart every woman is a bourgeoisie—and you prove it. (*To* CHRIS.) Right?
CHRIS: Right.
BILL (*to* JANET): That's what you are . . . a misguided little bourgeois bit!
CHRIS: You're ashamed of us! (*Right of* JANET.)
BILL: We're not good enough for you! (*Left of* JANET.)
CHRIS: What would your mother say if she could see now? (*He steps over back of settee so that* MIL *is pushed away.*)
BILL: We've seduced you——
CHRIS: Loved you——
BILL: Bedded you——
CHRIS: Wedded you——
BILL: Tumbled you——
CHRIS: Rumbled you——
BILL: Humbled you——
CHRIS: Stripped you——
BILL: Whipped you——
CHRIS: Kissed and caressed you——
BILL: Taken your virginity away from you——
BILL ⎱ (*together loudly*): And you don't bloody well appreciate
CHRIS ⎰ us! Bugger you!
(*Pause.*)
MIL (*coming above them behind the settee*): Look . . . I don't want to cause any trouble——
(*He breaks off.* CHRIS *and* BILL *look at him with exaggerated curiosity.*)
BILL: You're welcome——

24

CHRIS: As the flowers in Spring.
BILL: To Phil the Fluters balls!
JANET (*to* MIL): They've been like it ever since they saw some play at the Rep. Take a lot of no notice.
MIL: I meant I don't want to come between you and—— (*Hesitates.*)
BILL (*solemnly*): We are only married in the flesh—men . . . even Americans . . . can put us asunder.
JANET: I just asked him round because he seemed lonely.
BILL (*as to a child*): There's a good girl. . . . (*To* MIL.) She really has a soft heart. Hasn't she got a soft heart, Chris?
CHRIS: She has . . . it goes with her head.
JANET: You'll get a bloody great lump on yours if you don't shut up. (*To* MIL.) You must admit you looked like a spare part in the Kicking Horse last night.
BILL: As a matter of fact I thought you were looking for pot.
(MINNIE *comes in. She is dressed and wears a mini dress and patterned stockings.*)
MINNIE: Ray moved fast, didn't he?
BILL: This isn't Ray's bonanza. Chris drew his savings from the Post Office.
MINNIE: Has he been holding out on us?
CHRIS: I only just found the key . . . (*He takes a screwdriver from his pocket and waves it about.*) . . . to my strong box.
MINNIE: I told you he was a genius, didn't I?
MIL: None of you take drugs, do you?
JANET: You don't have to take them seriously.
MINNIE: I'll have some toast, Mav. Hey Mav . . . you all right?
(MAV *is sitting by the stove. Quite still.*)
Mav!
MAV (*coming to*): Sorry . . . I was day dreaming.
BILL (*loudly*): What's happened to the commissariat?
MAV: Nothing . . . I'm quite all right.
(RAY *pushes open the door and staggers in loaded with groceries.*)
RAY (*posing triumphantly*): Yuk-Yuk.
BILL: It's Mother Courage herself . . . give a cheer, children.

(MINNIE *points to* CHRIS's *provisions and blows a raspberry at* RAY.)

RAY (*eyeing the table*): Did Father Christmas drop in or what?

MIL (*indicating* CHRIS): He robbed a call box.

RAY (*to* CHRIS): Bloody silly. They're having them watched now.
(CHRIS *shrugs and eats*.)

JANET: How did you get yours?

RAY: Borrowed it. (*To* MAV *with food*.) I'd like two boiled eggs, toast, marmalade and coffee. (*Puts down items*.)
(MAV *gets up*.)

MINNIE (*to* MAV): You sit down. I'll feed the brute.

RAY: What's up?

MAV: It's just the cold I think . . . getting up.

MINNIE: Go and sit by the fire——

MAV: I'm all right.

MINNIE: Do as you're told. Have a ciggy in the warm . . . go on.
(BILL *goes off*.)

RAY (*producing a new pack*): Here y'are. King size.

MINNIE: Go on . . . hoppit, I'll bring you food and drinkies. That's what you need.

MAV (*smiling*): I'm quite all right really.

RAY: Let her slave. Make a change to see her doing something.

MINNIE: Belt up you, or you'll get your eggs addled.
(MAV *moves to the chair by the fire*.)

JANET: Like an aspirin?

MAV: I'll just sit.

RAY (*returning to beside* CHRIS): If you want to do a job make it a big 'un.
(BILL *comes back in carrying some clay and a modelling board. He sets them on the sideboard or on a table he uses for working*.)

CHRIS: I got what I wanted.

JANET: Who'd you borrow it off?

RAY: You.

JANET: Oh very funny!

BILL: Are you all hanging on in here or do I get a chance to work?

MIL (*to* JANET): He told me you wanted to borrow two quids.

RAY: Quid.
MIL: Didn't you ask him?
BILL (*loudly, leaning on table*): I'm glad everyone is paying attention to what I say!
RAY: Go away you funny little man.
BILL (*to* CHRIS): Did you hear what he called me?
CHRIS: Ignore him. He's frustrated.
BILL: Flagellated.
CHRIS: Desiccated.
BILL: Amputated.
CHRIS: Truncated.
BILL: Castrated.
CHRIS: Masticated.
BILL: Infibulated.
  (CHRIS *stops.*)
CHRIS: In what?
BILL: Chastity belted.
RAY: If you mean I have belted my chastity, you are right. I belt it nightly, brightly, tritely, uprightly—and if I lay hands on the author of that bloody play I'd belt him too for stuffing that in your nuts.
JANET: Hear hear!
BILL (*to* MIL): I hope you appreciate genius.
MIL: When I can recognize it.
BILL: You don't see it here?
MIL: I'm not literary, I guess. Just honest.
  (*Pause. The men look at each other.*)
RAY: He's upset about his two quids.
BILL (*to* MIL): Look upon it as part of your Foreign Aid Programme.
MINNIE (*putting food before* RAY): Here—get stuffed with this.
JANET: And give him back any change you got.
RAY: You're joking, of course.
JANET: I'm not—it's his and you got it under false pretences.
RAY: I mean you're joking thinking there is any.
BILL (*meaningly*): But you've got to pay him back, see.
RAY: 'Course I will.
BILL: On your Moslemic honour?

RAY: On my own personal Torah.

BILL: Your Buddhic Tope?

JANET: Oh don't start that again! You're like a couple of stale comics with it.

MINNIE: They're narked at your bringing a new male into the fold.

BILL (*stopping*): She's right! (*To* MIL.) It's a free house. Help yourself.

MIL: I just thought Janet might like a day at the Zoo.
(*Pause. All look at each other.*)

JANET: The Zoo?

MIL: There's one out of the town I hear . . . with a castle.

CHRIS: He means Dudley.

JANET: I'm not traipsing out there.

RAY: Who the hell wants to visit a zoo this weather?

MINNIE (*coming in with a cup of coffee and food for* MAV): I wouldn't mind—what about you, Mav?

MAV: No thank you.

BILL (*to* MIL): Looks like you've lost out.

MIL: I was only asking Janet.

BILL: Take one, pal, take all.

MIL (*rises*): Well—I guess that's done then.

BILL (*pushing* MIL *down again*): We could go in the Spring. Unless you're in a hurry.

MIL: I don't see why one should wait until Spring to visit a zoo.

BILL: True lovers love the Spring.

CHRIS: When birds do sing . . . hey ding a ding a ding——

BILL (*with simulated amazement*): He doesn't know.

RAY: Get on——

CHRIS: We've all got a lot to learn.

BILL: Shall we tell him?

RAY: Let's——

CHRIS: Let's——

BILL: All together now.
(*They begin to beat time and then start to dance a Shepherd's Hey.* BILL *and* MINNIE *start it.*)

ALL: It was a lover and his lass. . . .
With a hey and a ho and a hey. . . . Noninoni.

(They go through "It was a lover" getting very boisterous. The girls join in the dance and sing. MIL *sits apart. At its height* JANET *grabs his hand and he joins in.)*
(They are dancing in a circle and singing as . . .)

CURTAIN

END OF ACT ONE

ACT TWO

When the curtain rises CHRIS *is on stage. He is sitting at the table with his feet on it strumming a guitar or banjo. Every now and then he stops to consult the "Teach Yourself" book, with "First Steps" on the cover. He is not competent with the instrument in any way.*

After a moment MAV *comes in. She is on her way to the kitchen to put the kettle on.*

CHRIS: Feeling better?
MAV: It's gone now. Funny.
CHRIS: Maybe you should take yourself to a doctor.
MAV: I'd feel a fool. I just got dizzy for a bit, that's all.
CHRIS: I could make a song about that. "I got dizzy for a bit about you".
MAV: If you could play you might.
CHRIS: "But when I got my senses back baby,
 When I got my senses back baby,
 I knew it couldn't be true!"
 (*He picks a note here and there.*)
 "'Cos what do you want with a shower like me?"
 (*Strikes a heavy chord.*)
 "Hurry up Mav with that bloody cup of tea!"
MAV: You could have made one yourself.
CHRIS: I was lost in creating. (*Strums a chord.*)
MAV: Do you think you'll ever get hold of that?
CHRIS: Buggered if I know. (*Stretches.*) But if the Stones do it why shouldn't I?
MAV: They're educated. A levels all over the place.
CHRIS: Gerraway!
MAV: I read it somewhere.
CHRIS: I used to get told to shut up at school. There was this

teacher called Gower. We used to call him Old In Off. "Thank you, Caruso," he used to say, "but in your case silence is golden. Keep your trap shut."

MAV: He sounds a right birk.

CHRIS: He wasn't bad . . . always playing pocket billiards . . . that's why we called him "In off".

MAV: I don't get it.

CHRIS: He'd put his hand in his pocket and he'd be off, see?

MAV: Off what?

CHRIS: Off. Playing pocket billiards! There's a lot of 'em do it. (*A door slams off. Voices.*)
Hello, the herd's back.

MAV: I can hear Bill didn't like it.

CHRIS: Does he ever?

(*The door opens and* BILL *enters with* MIL, MINNIE, JANET *and* RAY.)

BILL: . . . it's the cranes . . . the cranes are the ones you want to watch. They're bloody marvellous. Ever seen them?

MIL: No I don't——

BILL: You haven't lived, boy! They come swooping down, see. (BILL *imitates a crane coming in to land. Throughout the following he and the others who join him maintain the imitated stance of the cranes with bent knees and flapping hands.*)
And sort of bow . . . (*Grabs* JANET'*s hand.*) . . . to his chosen bit and then jumps . . . (*He jumps up.*) . . . and round. . . . (*Pirouettes.*) (*To* JANET.) Get stuck in, gel! You bow and hop remember . . . you've seen it. . . .
(JANET *joins him in the movement.* MINNIE *and* RAY *take it up too.*)
Round and up and bow and hop, now left, now right, now the neck bit . . . dad dada dad dada dad dad dada! (*All four are now gravely hopping and dancing.*) The minuet bit. . . . (*They dance this bit in silence.*) Then he's on the job!
(BILL *attacks* JANET, RAY *attacks* MINNIE. *Both the girls scream and all fall over on the floor.*)

MINNIE: Oy, oy . . . lay off——

JANET: Not here, you birk!
   (*The girls struggle free.*)
BILL (*to* MIL): See what I mean? When it comes to mating they got us homo sapiente licked ... see us getting wound up for a jump on the greensward as Nature intended and we'd get nicked per ardua ad quicker! (*With a complete change of tone to* MAV.) Oh, you survived then?
MAV: Just about.
MINNIE: You ought to see a doctor.... (*Sees tea.*) Oh goodie ... is there a cup left?
MAV: You had a good time then? (*Pours tea.*)
MINNIE: Not bad.
BILL: We should have waited till the Spring ... he'd have seen them all at it then.
RAY: You're a right randy, you are.
BILL: I have an academic interest in procreative rites.
RAY: What about that bit in the caff? She was procreative all right.
JANET: They were all trying to see up her skirt.
RAY: She was on one of them bar stools ... you know——
MINNIE: Lecherous lot. (*Drinks tea.*)
JANET: She went all red when she saw them looking.
RAY: We were on low chairs see ... cor!
JANET: She was wearing white locknit knickers and the elastic was too tight.
CHRIS: All right, you can push your eyes back——
BILL: She was, in short, a typical unkempt bit of English bindweed.
MIL: I thought she looked rather nice.
   (*Pause. They look at him.*)
   Well dressed. Nicely made up.
   (*Pause.*)
BILL: He always disagrees with me—have you noticed?
MIL: I expect we've got different tastes.
BILL: I wouldn't describe what you like as taste at all.
JANET: Leave him alone, Bill. You're always at him.
BILL: Not sexual or territorial I assure you. I am trying to lead him into the way of truth and light. God knows he needs it.

MINNIE: If I was him I'd dot you one.

RAY: Oy, oy! We want no threats of violence here.

CHRIS (*loud strum on guitar*): "Hey hey we're the monkeys".

BILL (*to* MINNIE): By their fruits shall ye know them. There is a strain of Hun in you. You're always wanting someone to hit someone.

MINNIE: There's a whole hog in you . . . you'll eat anything.

JANET: He had two fruit parfaits and a bar of chocolate in the caff.

BILL: I enjoy food.

RAY: You don't have to listen to yourself enjoying.

MINNIE: It's the hog coming through. They chomp chomp.

RAY: That's just it . . . chomp chomp.

JANET: It's more sucking . . . a sort of slurp.

MINNIE: Exactly . . . like a hog.

BILL: The hog is a fastidious clean living animal brutalized by contact with our smelly human civilization. I am proud and happy to be associated with the hog.

MIL: Eating sweet things is a depressive symptom.

BILL: I've got a depressive symptom for you. (*Picks up clay model of a sphere.*) See that? Recognize that?

MIL: Looks like a cinder.

BILL: A cinder . . . correct. That is the world to be. I had intended to call it "Mao Tse Tung Thought Here" but I've changed my mind . . . it shall be called "An American Passed By".

MIL: Can't be me. I'm a pacifist.

BILL: I didn't specify the American.

MIL: A nod's as good as a wink, Bill.

MINNIE: I'm glad you passed by . . . if you hadn't we'd be pigging it on the N.A.

RAY: It's a great life——

MIL: What do you do when my money runs out?

BILL: We adopt our Micawber stance and wait for something to turn up.

MIL: And if something doesn't?

BILL (*to* CHRIS): Would you mind shifting your great clodhopping earth shakers?

(CHRIS *moves his feet from the table.* BILL *sits.*)
As President of the Chamber of Commerce I move that
Minnie the Moaner gets supper.
MINNIE: Get stuffed.
BILL: Opportunity is a fine thing. Lady Godiva then.
(*He looks across at* JANET.)
JANET: I thought we were going down the Kicking Horse.
RAY: I'd sooner do a pub. A bloody good booze up would suit me.
BILL: You're disgusting when you're drunk.
RAY: So I should hope.
BILL: You'd be better off on pot. It doesn't smell.
(CHRIS *twangs his guitar.*)
Perhaps Sergovia ought to take a turn.
CHRIS: At what?
BILL: Cooking supper.
CHRIS: You were going to fetch fish and chips back.
(*Pause.* BILL *looks round.*)
BILL: Is that as big a shock to you lot as it is to me?
MIL: It's my fault. I promised him and it slipped my mind.
BILL: Oh . . . I find it hard to believe you'd handle fish and chips even if you recognized them.
MIL: I'm not that dumb about England, Bill.
BILL: But you wouldn't want to dirty your hygienically educated Transatlantic paws with a greasy mess of fried huss and chips in the Daily Dirt. You'd want them iced, frozen, hermetically sealed, deoderized and bland. Bland! The epitaph of the last Empire of the West, the end of the Great American Dream . . . a bland corpse!
MIL (*laughing*): You're a great guy, Bill!
BILL: In the zoo I am the boss cat.
MIL: Who's arguing.
CHRIS (*loudly*): I am! Who's getting the nosh?
(*Pause. All look at one another.*)
MIL: O.K. . . . O.K. I guess it's my pigeon.
RAY: No point in our going. We're skint.
MIL (*getting up*): What about that florin of yours?
RAY: Ask him (BILL.) about his box.

BILL (*as* MIL *turns*): Help yourself. We've got a cupboard he's worried about too.
CHRIS (*loud*): I'm starving.
MIL: What's in it?
BILL: No key . . . but his florin's round his neck.
RAY: It's a private heirloom.
MIL: I thought everything was common property here.
BILL: It'll be fish and chips six times—seven if you intend to sample part of our national dish. And I'm not referring to Janet.
MIL: O.K.
MAV: Plenty of vinegar for me. Whoosh it on.
MIL: Sure. Keep batting, Bill.
   (MIL *goes out. Pause.*)
BILL (*with distaste*): Keep batting! Do I look like a bloody cricketer?
MAV: He's got you weighed up.
BILL: I was weighed up, packed up and despatched before he got rid of his umbilical.
RAY: Where to?
BILL: Christ knows. (*He picks up a wad of clay and begins to model it.*)
MAV: I don't want to sound a misery but we've got to decide where we're going.
RAY: Right up the sodding spout, I'd say.
MAV: Oh, Ray!
MINNIE: It's as good a place as anywhere.
CHRIS: Right up the spout with the dirt in me mouth. (*Twang.*)
RAY: You can pack that in.
CHRIS: You know a better way of making money?
RAY: What you make with that is carache.
CHRIS (*exaggerated, playful*): Watch it! (*He aims the guitar at* RAY.)
RAY: You're a dead man, Baxter!
   (RAY *tilts back on his chair.*)
CHRIS: Yeah?
RAY: Yeah . . . them's fighting words.
   (*He lifts his foot and jerks up the guitar. He lunges forward*

and he and CHRIS *mock fight. They fall near* MINNIE.)

MINNIE: Pack it in, will yerh! (*Gets up from her chair to avoid them.*)

RAY (*looking up from the floor,* CHRIS *is above him*): I never knew you had red drawers. (*Grabs* MINNIE'*s legs.*)

MINNIE (*trying to get free*): Well now you do, go and play somewhere else.

RAY (*to* CHRIS): Did you know about them? (*Points up* MINNIE'*s skirt.*)

MINNIE (*her voice rising*): Pack it up! (*She tries to free herself.*)

CHRIS: Very tasty I must say——

(MINNIE *struggles, giggling and oohing.*)

MINNIE: Will you let go . . . here, help me, you two.

JANET: Sit on 'em, Min.

(RAY *and* CHRIS *pull* MINNIE *down rolling apart so that she lands between them, then with a quick movement each grabs one of her legs and stands up.* MINNIE *is now upended with her skirts hanging down displaying her underwear. She screams.*)

RAY: And what's offered for this prime bit of pork? (*Slaps* MINNIE'*s bottom.*)

MINNIE: Oooooooooooh! Lemme go . . . lemme go will you!

CHRIS: Quiet or we slap it.

RAY: Hard . . . right here!

(*He slaps* MINNIE *on her bottom. She yells.* MIL *comes back through the door. He stops dead.*)

Here y'are . . . want a go . . . dollar a do!

(MIL *moves across the room. Grabs* RAY *and* CHRIS'*s arms and wrenches them apart so that they loose* MINNIE *and let her fall.*)

Hey . . . steady on——

CHRIS: Watch it!

(MINNIE *scrambles up.*)

MINNIE: You are a couple of cows! (*Smooths down her clothes.*)

MIL (*to* BILL): Couldn't you help her?

BILL: She likes it.

CHRIS: She loves it.

RAY: Gives her an appetite for fish and chips.

(MIL *looks at* MINNIE.)

MINNIE: Didn't you get them?
MIL: There's a man downstairs asking for Chris. I think he's a cop.
(*Pause.*)
BILL: Is he in uniform?
MIL: No but there's a car with police on it outside.
(BILL, CHRIS *and* RAY *go to the window.*)
MAV: Is it a police car?
RAY: What's the betting it's that kiosk you did?
CHRIS: Ah get . . . how'd they know about that?
MINNIE: We can give him an alibi . . . he never left here.
(*Kisses him.*) Don't you fret.
CHRIS (*going to door*): If I can't fool a dick I deserve to be jugged.
(CHRIS *goes out.*)
RAY: What a waste. It's the same risk for a big job.
JANET (*alarmed*): He won't have to go to prison will he?
MAV (*to* BILL): Well, will he?
BILL: He doesn't seem worried.
MAV: That's not an answer.
BILL: It's the only one I've got. . . . (*To* MIL.) We'll still have to eat.
MIL: Do I get some for Chris or not?
BILL: If he's not here we'll share 'em.
MIL: If he goes to jail will you share that?
(MIL *goes out.*)
RAY: He's getting cheeky!
MAV: Still he's right. It's one thing we can't share.
JANET: I don't want to, thank you very much.
MINNIE: They won't get Chris—he's too smart. He's quiet but he's smart.
RAY (*to* MINNIE): You be quiet and give me a drag.
JANET: Here. (*She pushes a packet towards him.*)
(BILL *leaves his work and goes to the window. Looks out.*)
RAY (*picking up cig.*): These all you got? (*American pack.*) Can't look a gift horse, I suppose.
MAV: If we did we'd be in Queer St. Ten days now he's fed us, kept us in fags . . . food, everything but sleep with us.

MINNIE: It cost him a bomb today.
RAY: He's a funny cuss, no kidding.
BILL (*coming back to the table*): It wasn't a cop.
MAV: How do you know?
BILL: The car's gone off but no one got in it.
(RAY *goes to the door and looks out.*)
MAV: Have you got any ideas?
BILL (*picking up clay*): I'm building a new world—it'll be pear shaped and called Maison de Gaulle.
MAV: What are we going to do about Mil?
BILL: I shall let him live and hope for mercy.
MAV: We can't expect to live off him much longer.
BILL (*to* JANET): Has he had you yet?
JANET: You kidding? I think he's a virgin.
MINNIE: If you expect Janet to play around the houses with him just for feeding stuffs I'm out for one.
BILL: I never said——
MINNIE (*high for once*): We're not running a knocking shop!
RAY (*returning*): That fellow down there's no cop.
BILL: I said he wasn't.
JANET: I don't think he knows anything about it.
RAY: Who? What do you mean? I've known more cops'n you've had hot dinners.
JANET: I'm talking about Mil.
MINNIE: Old squashy balls here's hinting that he's keeping us for a chance with Janet.
RAY: Well ain't he?
   (*Pause.*)
   Come on now—tell me why he is then.
   (*Pause.*)
JANET: He went very gentlemanly over you upending her. Seeing her knickers.
BILL: He is a conventional middle-class Yankee Doodle Dandyo sniffing round for a sample of our English swingingness.
RAY: In short a dirty young transatlantic git. (*Looks at fag.*) These burn out easy, don't they?
MINNIE: Here. (*Tosses him matches.*)
MAV: The fact remains, we're living on him——

RAY: Not completely. The air is free and the rent's not paid.
MAV: Nobody does anything any more. Nobody tries anything.
   (CHRIS *comes from the landing door.*)
MINNIE: You're getting a ripe old wailer, Mav. We're all right
   ... what's to worry?
MAV: If he decamps tomorrow how do we eat?
BILL (*to* CHRIS): It wasn't a cop then?
CHRIS: Quite right. It wasn't a cop. (*Takes off jacket and hangs it up.*)
MAV: I repeat—if he packs up how do we eat?
RAY: Wiv our mouves ... same as usual. (MAV *turns away.*) All right all right ... just a joke.
JANET: Honest Mav I don't see what you're going on about. We always managed before.
CHRIS: And we shall manage again.
MINNIE: It isn't as if he minds or as if we'd asked for that matter.
CHRIS: He loves it here. (*Goes off to bedroom.*)
RAY: Can't keep him away——
MINNIE: He's lonely I think——
JANET: I think he likes being in a crowd ... friendly.
MINNIE: He's a long way from home. He must miss it.
BILL: According to Janet he hasn't had it to miss.
MINNIE: Oh you ... a right randy old birk you're going to be.
BILL: He came to take Janet to the zoo ... she attracted him.
RAY: And with every reason ... she's a delicious bit of Rumplestiltskin, aren't you, ducky?
   (RAY *claps his hands and kneels on the settee on which* JANET *is sitting. Grips her on either side of the waist with his hands and squeezes.* JANET *writhes and giggles.*)
JANET (*shrieking*): Don't do that ... oooh stop it!
RAY: She's a lovely bit!
JANET (*shrieking*): Ray don't ... oooh ... it's making me weak.
   (*She slides down the settee with* RAY *coming on top of her. Her feet come off the floor, her skirt is rucked up revealing all of her thighs.*)
RAY: Grrrrrrrrhh.

JANET: Ooooooh . . . Ray! Ow. . . . (*He kisses her round the neck and nuzzles her ear.*) Ooooooh . . . stop . . . I like it. (*They subside into necking.* CHRIS *comes in and stands watching them. He takes a packet of English cigarettes from his pocket and opens it.*)
CHRIS: It's nice to see young people happy, isn't it?
MINNIE: Here . . . where'd you get them?
CHRIS: What?
MINNIE: Them . . . them Players . . . you pinched his florin?
CHRIS (*holds up cigs.*): Gift from a pal of mine. (*Tosses her a cig.*) Enjoy it. (*Turns to* MAV.) Mav?
MAV: Ta.
(*He tosses one to her.*)
I must say it's nice to see one of these again for a change.
MINNIE: Ah . . . them Americans are like Turkish . . . better'n nothing though.
MAV: We ought to decide something . . . we ought to have a plan.
BILL: I don't think I'll call it Maison de Gaulle. I think I'll call it—— (*He eyes it.*)
CHRIS: You don't want to worry, Mav.
BILL (*to* MINNIE): What shall I call it?
MINNIE (*eyeing the clay*): Looks like a pear drop.
CHRIS: Or a sawn off testicle.
MINNIE: Uhhh! (*She pulls a face in simulated pain.*)
MAV: He can't be that conventional if——
JANET (*slapping* RAY'*s hand which has crept up her thigh*): Oh no you don't!
RAY: You know you love it.
MAV: He can't be that conventional if——
JANET: Not now I don't—— (*She struggles.*)
RAY: Oh . . . come on . . . Chris. (*He nods over at* CHRIS *who moves over to help him.*)
JANET: Ah . . . no . . . Min . . . stop him.
MINNIE: You help yourself. I had to.
(CHRIS *has grabbed* JANET. *She screams and giggles.*)
MAV (*shouting*): Will you shut up! Shut up!
(*Everyone stares at* MAV.)

RAY (*with exaggerated incredulity*): Eh?
MAV: I've been trying to say something for the last five minutes.
RAY: Then you say it, love . . . go on . . . get it off your chest.
(*Pause.*) Go on.
MAV: He can't be that conventional if he's here to get out of going to Vietnam.
(*Pause.* CHRIS *and* RAY *exchange glances.*)
RAY (*shrugging*): Beats me.
BILL: I shall call it "The Good Shepherd U.S.A.".
CHRIS: Why U.S.A.?
BILL: Because like all good Shepherds it feeds you, fattens you and in the end slaughters you. All in the interest of profit.
(*The door opens and* MIL *comes in with a large parcel of fish and chips.*)
MIL: They sure smell good. (*He dumps the package on the table.*)
BILL: Watch it! (*He grabs his model, misses and the chips go on it.*)
MIL: Gee . . . sorry. (*Touches* BILL *who shrugs him off, removes his almost flattened model and goes off.*)
MINNIE: Never mind his muck. Let's have 'em.
(MINNIE *takes the packet and starts to open it.*)
MIL (*to* CHRIS): Was it a cop?
CHRIS: Can they pick you up over here for not going to Vietnam?
MIL: Not the way things are. (*Goes to kitchen and gets plate etc.*)
MINNIE: Here Mav. . . . (*Tosses packet to* MAV.) I think he's drowned them!
MIL: She said to whoosh it on.
MAV: Well, you certainly whooshed.
CHRIS: What do you mean the way things are?
MIL: The present state of the law.
CHRIS: How's it work then?
MIL: Aw it's all involved . . . to do with how the draft works.
(BILL *enters.*)
MINNIE: Catch, gutsy!
(MINNIE *throws the packet of fish and chips to* BILL *who catches them.* MIL *comes to her for his. She takes plate etc. from him and plonks the packet in his hands.*)

MIL: You just eat them with your fingers, huh?
MINNIE: What's the bottle?
MIL (*taking bottle from pocket*): I thought some wine'd go down with them.
RAY: You want beer with chips.
JANET: I don't. Wine'll do me.
RAY: That's promising—— (*He slaps her thigh.*)
JANET: Oh . . . lay off! (*Brushes her stockings.*) You're all greasy.
MINNIE: You can say that again . . . all over.
RAY: Hey, watch it.
MIL: Shall we pass it round?
MINNIE (*pointing to* RAY): Him last then . . . he'd have the lot.
RAY (*phlegmatically*): Balls!
MIL: You start it, Mav . . . ladies first.
(*During the following the bottle goes round.*)
BILL: Can't you be a conscientious objector in America?
(*Pause.* MIL *looks at* BILL.)
MIL: I'd have thought you know all the answers about the States, Bill.
BILL: The question was about you. (*Eats a chip.*)
MIL: Gee, you're a hair splitter! You'd be a big hit on one of them TV programmes . . . you know where they try to get some poor guy into a corner.
BILL: How poor do you have to be to keep seven on fish and chips and Beaujolais?
MIL: Eat, drink and be merry—tomorrow I may be broke.
MAV: We don't want your cash.
MIL: I'm loaded really.
RAY (*to* MINNIE *who now has the bottle*): You going to drain that? (*Grabs the bottle.*)
MINNIE: I've only had a mouthful.
RAY: Some mouth! (*Pulls at bottle.*)
MINNIE: It's Janet next anyhow.
MIL (*taking bottle from them*): Yeah, it's Janet.
(*Pause.*)
RAY: I was gonna pass it to her.
MIL: Sure you were but I don't want it spilt.

BILL: Waste not and thou shalt not want.
MIL: And all things come to he who waits. Right?
BILL: Including measles, mumps, halitosis, the pox and a bullet with your name on it.
MIL: That's a bright outlook.
CHRIS: He's always been a bloody optimist he has.
BILL: I take after my dad . . . he was a newsreader with the B.B.C. till he committed suicide after his nine o'clock spasm.
JANET: You told me he was a roadsweeper.
BILL: That was before Carleton Greene spotted him. They were looking for a man who could (BILL *puts a long chip into his mouth and sucks it in through pursed lips so that it slides in like a snake.*) read the news without weeping or laughing. My father was incapable of either. He was not only a roadsweeper you see . . . he was also a bachelor. He had, in short, a touch of the Ted Heaths.
MINNIE: Bloody liar.
JANET: Who's next?

(RAY *makes a grab for the bottle.* CHRIS *takes it.*)

MIL: And what was the news that finished him?
BILL: I was thinking, if it wasn't the cops who called on you, Chris, what was the cop's car doing outside?
CHRIS: That's a question. (*He takes the bottle away from his mouth.* RAY *grabs at it.*) Don't be bloody impatient.
RAY: I'm gasping.
CHRIS: Suck your chips . . . there's juice on them.
BILL: Could it be the C.I.A. is interested?

(MIL *intercepts the bottle as it passes from* CHRIS *to* RAY. *Holds it out to* BILL.)

MIL: Your turn. (*He touches* BILL *who reacts.*)
RAY (*to* MIL): Sod you!
MAV: Ray!
RAY: Now don't come the right little mother . . . he's having me on!
MAV: It's his bottle.
BILL (*coldly for* MIL's *sake*): When he brings it in here it's not.

(BILL *tosses the bottle to* RAY, *keeping it upright but some of it still spills from the top.*)

JANET. Here, watch it! You've wet my dress.
RAY: Take it off then.
JANET: It's not that wet.
RAY: Pity . . . how's that.
   (RAY *empties a drop more wine on to* JANET's *dress.*)
JANET: What you do that for?
RAY: Obvious . . . you got my passion up. (*Grabs her.*)
JANET (*pushing him off*): Me? I'd have been raped if Mav hadn't chipped in. Wouldn't I, Min?
MINNIE: Gawd help us tonight when he's got that down him!
MIL (*putting hand on bottle*): Would you rather he didn't?
RAY: Don't be bloody silly——
MIL: But if you get violent.
RAY: I don't get violent . . . do I?
CHRIS: He gets unbearable.
MINNIE: Inexcusable.
JANET: Inexhaustible.
MIL (*taken aback*): Oh . . . I see.
RAY: They love it.
BILL: Get him really drunk . . . then he's incapable.
RAY: Not on your bloody nellie I'm not.
JANET: I'll have to change this. . . . (*She squeezes her dress.*) It's all clammy.
RAY: I'll give you a hand—— (*Puts his hand up her skirt.*)
JANET: Oh pack it in—— (*She slaps his hand and goes off.*)
RAY (*to* MIL): Go on, you help her.
MAV: Behave yourself, Ray.
BILL: And pass the bottle, you've had your lot.
RAY (*to* MAV): Bin getting a bit conscience stricken lately . . . haven't you, Mav?
MAV: Don't be silly.
RAY (*to* CHRIS): Hasn't she been getting like a wet week?
CHRIS: I never met a wet week.
RAY: She's been on about where what's coming from tomorrow—now she's getting all speak nice and keep the sheets clean . . . what's that got to do with us?
MINNIE: You leave Mav alone.

RAY: She's getting middle-aged about it. (*To* MIN.) Where you off to?

MINNIE: Don't be personal. When you gotta go, you gotta go! (*She goes off.*)

MAV: Take the bottle off him.

RAY: I bet you weren't sick . . . I bet you didn't come to the zoo 'cos you might have seen a thing or two you'd have blushed at.

BILL: The way you were behaving even I blushed.

RAY: Why shouldn't he help 'em change?

MIL: Because I don't want to.

RAY: Aw come on . . . you ought to know us now. You don't have to do any act here. We don't mind you making a pass at Janet.

MIL: I don't want to make a pass . . . at Janet.

RAY: He's a right bourgeoisie en he? (*To* MIL.) Come on . . . shake down . . . let yourself go. Have a ball.

BILL: The Mayflower rotted years ago. The C.I.A. has taken over.

MIL: I'm not that keen on the C.I.A. either.

RAY: They wouldn't show up in a British Police car, would they? (*Snaps his fingers.*) Disguised!

MIL: You guys are all too serious. The C.I.A.'s nothing to do with me . . . and it doesn't waste time hunting little draft dodgers anywhere.

BILL: Still, there was a police car looking us over.

RAY (*about* MIL): Maybe he did some big job and is lying low here.

MIL: Look I tell you——

BILL: You don't have to worry . . . we don't love the law either.

RAY: Show me a cop and I'll show you a louse.

BILL: But we've got them tied up in this town.

RAY: Name what you want——

BILL: Forged passport——

RAY: Safe hideaway——

BILL: Good fence——

RAY: Guns——

BILL: Anything——

RAY: From a luger to a tank——
BILL: From a lawyer to a lady——
RAY: You name it——
BILL: We got it——
RAY: And you can have it.
BILL: Straight. I've got it all in my box.
(*They lean over* MIL.)
MAV: Leave him alone.
BILL: We are offering help. A Christian thought in these pagan times.
MAV: We can't go on living off him. It's not fair.
MIL: You're welcome. I'm glad to help tide you over.
RAY (*serious*): But is the loot hot?
MIL: What's that?
BILL (*with drama*): Is it . . . honest?
MIL (*rolls his chip paper into a ball*): Sure it's honest. Do I look like a crook?
MAV: Of course he doesn't.
BILL: He doesn't look like a kooky liberal pacifist either.
MIL (*laughing*): Could be I'm not. Could be I'm just a plain honest to God coward.
(MINNIE *and* JANET *come on. They are now wearing bell-bottomed double-breasted trouser suits. They dance on arms round each other saying "Sock it to me, sock it to me". They halt in the middle of the room and pose, asking for applause.*)
BILL: I read somewhere that when the female begins to be indistinguishable from the male it is a sign of approaching extinction.
MINNIE: The sooner you're extinct the better, mate. Like 'em, Mav?
RAY: A skirt's more convenient.
JANET: These are safer.
RAY (*going to her*): Since when have you wanted to be safe?
JANET: Keep off. . . . (*He bends over her on the arm of the chair.*) You'll wear me out.
RAY: Take more'n me to do that.
CHRIS: What about the elephant?

(*They all look at him.* BILL *at* RAY's *bottom which is up in the air as he kisses* JANET. RAY *turns his head slowly.*)

BILL: Are you being personal?

CHRIS: You can't tell one from the other, can you?
(*Pause.*)

RAY: He means one end from the other. (*To* CHRIS.) The trunk's the thicker bit.

CHRIS: You know what I mean. . . . (*To* BILL.) What he said.

MIL: Telling the bull from the cow?

CHRIS: That's it.

RAY: If you'd have been at the zoo you'd have seen the difference.

MIL: What Bill says is not true.

BILL: He won't learn, will he?

RAY: Who wants to?

CHRIS: Learn what?

BILL: The fate of man.

MIL: Is what?

BILL: A bag of pods beneath a female belly.

CHRIS: Gerraway.

BILL: It'll come—so take your passion while you can.

RAY (*grabs* JANET): I'm ready, I'm willing, I'm able.

BILL: No future for the mini skirt.

ALL: Get on.

BILL: No titillation from a pair of thighs six inches from the amulet.

MINNIE: Oooooooh!

BILL (*grabbing* MAV): No pubic thrills from rubbing tum to tum.

CHRIS (*grabbing* MINNIE): Wowwow! (*They fall together on the floor.*)

BILL (*pulling* MAV *closer*): No exhausting nights or sexy afternoons.

ALL: Ooooh!
(MIL *picks up guitar and strums.*)

BILL: No petting or fretting. (*Bends over* MAV.) No kissing or caressing. Grrr!

MINNIE: We can't live without it.

BILL: No prostrate or retreat position. (*Dances slowly round* MAV.)

RAY: Oy, watch it!

BILL: No rounded bottoms. (*Cups* MAV's *bottom in his hands*.) And no sacred places——

ALL: Groan!

BILL: No diaphragms, no pills and no French letters.

MINNIE: What? No safety?

BILL (*stopping as he catches* MIL's *eye,* MAV *between them*): No love.

ALL: Oooooh no!

BILL: No passion.

CHRIS: What, none at all?

BILL: No, none!

RAY: There'll be a bloody revolution, mate!

BILL: Not revolution—evolution.

CHRIS: Science'll stop that . . . science can do anything nowadays.

RAY: He's right. It can make a man into a woman and vice versa.

MINNIE: I've never understood how they did that. I mean——

RAY: They graft it on.

JANET: What do they do the other way round?

RAY: Cut it off.

BILL: It's all in the mind anyway.

MIL: Is it, Bill?

BILL (*angry*): Ask your dad.

MIL: He's dead.

BILL: Yeah . . . well we've all got troubles. Keep playing.
(BILL *grabs* RAY *and* CHRIS. *Pulls them towards the door*.) C'mon——

RAY: What the——

CHRIS: I'm happy here——

BILL: C'mon.

CHRIS: }
RAY: } But what the——? Give over——

BILL: Do as Daddy says . . .! C'mon.
(BILL *pulls off the protesting* RAY *and* CHRIS.)

MINNIE: What's he up to now?

JANET: He nearly ripped my . . . You all right, Mav?

(MAV *has sat panting a little.*)

MAV: I don't seem to have much breath left.

MINNIE: It's that bloody Bill . . . like dancing with a hippy elephant.

JANET (*stretching out*): What about Ray? It wasn't his head that the wine went to.

MAV (*to* MIL): You must think we're mad.

(MIL *looks at her and shakes his head.*)

MINNIE: What's mad about us?

MAV: Ask him.

MINNIE (*to* MIL): What's he know about it? He's a born natural.

MAV: It's the world we live in.

JANET: You kiddin'.

MAV: He knows . . . ask him . . . he knows what I mean.

MIL: I'm a drop-out too you know.

MAV: I don't want to know . . . it's your business . . . but why're you keeping us? Why're you paying out without asking questions?

MIL: What's there to ask?

MAV (*angry*): It's our business to know why you keep us . . . keep us sitting happy. That's not right . . . he's not right to do that.

MINNIE: Hold it, Mav——

MAV: He shouldn't have come.

MINNIE: Mav, list——

JANET (*simultaneously*): Keep it down——

MAV: He's made it easy for them——

JANET: Mav!

MINNIE: Mav!

MAV: They'll leave us flat . . . flat. You'll see.

MIL: If it's any comfort I've enough to keep you all, all your lives.

MAV: But you won't, will you? You'll move on . . . you'll move on and where'll we be then? We'll be left. They won't care.

(BILL, CHRIS *and* RAY *come dancing on in mini skirts, no shoes.*)

BILL (*as they stop in a line, to* MIL): Tenderness, passion or punishment. Rubber, leather or whipping, all available ... what's it to be?

(MIL *throws down the guitar and walks off.*)

MAV (*angrily to* BILL): What did you do that for?

BILL (*in exaggerated innocence*): Me? That wasn't me. That was his New England conscience.

RAY (*American*): He was a nice guy.

JANET: I liked him.

MINNIE: I don't think he's for games much.

BILL: He was shy ... poor little feller!

CHRIS: Still he was loaded. I reckon he was rich.

MAV: What do we do now?

BILL (*making a dance movement*): A little divertissement, eh?

MAV: What in God's name will that solve?

BILL: What is there to solve? We are British and christian. The Good Lord will provide.

RAY: Halleluliah!

MAV: We will wake up with nothing——

BILL: Well, if it's what we went to bed with we can't grumble. C'mon—— (*Tosses round the blindfolds.*)

MAV: I'm not playing——

BILL: One play all play ... right.

MAV: I'm not——

BILL (*forcefully*): One play all play ... right?

(*He looks at the others. They nod.* MAV *puts on the blindfold reluctantly. All turn round three times and then begin to hunt each other. There are mistakes and giggles and laughter and much rolling over as each seeks whom he wants.* MAV *takes off her blindfold and sits apart.*)

(CHRIS *eventually takes* MINNIE *off, carrying her.* RAY *does ditto with* JANET. BILL *still seeks.* MAV *goes off.*)

(*The door opens.* MIL *comes in. He watches* BILL *searching. Waits till he is at centre on all fours. Moves over.* BILL *touches* MIL's *knee. Freezes.* MIL *lifts his blindfold.*)

MIL (*softly*): Hi!

BLACK AND CURTAIN

END OF ACT TWO

ACT THREE

The scene is the same. The next morning.

MIL *is asleep on the settee when the curtain rises. After a moment* MAV *comes in. Sees* MIL *on settee, pauses. Crosses to the kitchen and puts on the kettle. Comes back to the main room and starts to search for cigarettes. Finds bottle in* CHRIS's *coat, inspects it and puts it back. Finds cigarettes in another pocket. Returns to the kitchen and makes the tea.* MIL *wakes, watches her. After a while she sees him.*

MAV: You take this in the morning?
MIL: Ugh?
MAV: Tea.
MIL: Oh . . . well. Guess I can try.
MAV (*gives him cup*): Where's Bill?
MIL (*looks round room*): He's not here?
MAV: I can't find him.
MIL: I guess . . . maybe he went for a walk.
MAV: He hates walking.

(*Pause.* MIL *sips his tea.*)

MIL: Makes me feel quite English.
MAV: You came back last night then?
MIL: Yeah——
MAV: We just have games you know.
MIL: I shouldn't have run out like that.
MAV: Bill's got a funny way of saying things sometimes.
MIL: Yeah.

(*They sip in silence for a moment.*)

MAV: How'd you feel about the tea?
MIL: It's good.
MAV: Only you Americans only have coffee, don't you?
MIL: Waking up I usually have fruit juice.

MAV: We don't run to that I'm afraid.
MIL: You sure Bill's not through there?
MAV: I couldn't see him.
MIL: Maybe he's with one of the others.
MAV: No . . . he's not there.
MIL: The bathroom maybe?
MAV: He'll turn up anyway.
MIL: Sure, he's not a child.
MAV (*pause*): Would you like some breakfast?
MIL: You do all the cooking?
MAV: I like it.
MIL: Was it Bill started it?
    (MAV *looks at him.*)
    All this. . . . (*He waves a hand.*) What goes on here?
MAV: It's his flat.
    (MAV *picks up her cup and goes to the kitchen part. She refills her cup.* MIL *gets up and follows her.*)
MIL: You annoyed at my asking?
MAV (*indicating cup*): Want any more?
MIL (*handing over cup*): I'm becoming a convert.
    (MAV *pours tea.*)
    The others don't seem to worry the way you do.
MAV: Don't you worry over Vietnam?
MIL: I don't get the connection.
MAV: It's just getting in a mess there seems no way out of.
MIL: I don't reckon on ever going back to the States.
MAV: You're lucky.
MIL: It's my home—what's lucky about losing a home?
MAV: Being able to buy another one.
    (CHRIS *comes in from the bedroom.*)
CHRIS (*to* MIL): Oh, what did you do? Bring the milk?
MIL (*looking at watch*): It's past nine.
CHRIS: But you're out and about and far from home.
MAV: He was here last night.
CHRIS: Get on. . . . (*To* MIL.) You kip here?
    (MIL *nods at the settee.*)
    Got over your dander quick, didn't you?
MIL: Let not the sun go down on your wrath.

CHRIS (*supping tea*): You bin listening to Billy boy. (*To* MAV.) Is he in the Bog?
MAV: He's out altogether by the look of it.
CHRIS: What . . . you mean outside?
(MAV *nods.*)
In the morning air?
MAV: Well, he's not here.
CHRIS: Something must have hit him.
MIL: Has he never been out early before? For a walk or something?
CHRIS: You must be joking, mate! It takes houses to get him outa bed, and he likes exercise like I like starving.
(MINNIE *enters barefoot and coated.*)
Hey what do you know . . . gutsy's up and active.
MINNIE (*glaring*): You're asking for the chopper, you are.
CHRIS: Not you. Bill. He's out walking or something.
MINNIE: Well it's one way of keeping warm . . . what's up with the fire?
CHRIS: Try the switch. (*To* MAV.) You get stuck with him last night?
(MAV *shakes her head.*)
What, Ray?
MAV: I slept by myself.
MINNIE: Can I have a cup? (*Coming back from the fire.*) I'm icing up. (*Rubs herself.*)
CHRIS: Which reminds me. It's about time I had my whack of the overcoat.
MAV: Ray hogs it.
MINNIE: It's Janet gets it most of the time.
CHRIS: She's always in there first, that's why. Any sugar?
MIL: Don't you have blankets?
CHRIS: The overcoat's a bonus.
MINNIE: And this weather. . . . (*She returns to the fire.*) Chris! It's going out.
CHRIS: I got nothing.
(*They look at* MIL.)
MIL: Here. (*He flips over a coin.*)
MINNIE: Ta . . . shove it in, Chris. (*She tosses it over to* CHRIS.

To MIL.) Am I late or you early?

MAV: He slept here.

MINNIE: Oh . . . in here?

MAV: Use your loaf.

MINNIE: Quite one of the family now then.

MIL: I think I'll take a walk.

MINNIE: I can't tell you what that bit of red does to me. (*Settles in front of the fire.*) It's like a new life.

CHRIS: All it costs is money. Your money or your life.

MINNIE: If I was a millionaire, I'd have a man follow me round with one of these.

MAV: It's raining.

MINNIE (*to* CHRIS): Put the bucket on the landing.

MAV: Mil said he was going for a walk.

MIL: I have to look in at my flat . . . see if there's anything.

CHRIS: Anything what?

MIL: . . . Mail . . . Letters . . . You know.

CHRIS (*between* MIL *and the door. Holding bucket*): You get many?

MIL: Now and then . . . I like to keep in touch.

MINNIE: I haven't had a letter in months.

(CHRIS laughs.)

You're getting very vulgar.

CHRIS: I never said a word.

MINNIE: You don't have to. You're getting a laugh like a dirty story.

MIL: I'll be back later.

(CHRIS *opens the door.*)

CHRIS: Seats at ten shillings . . . standing at six.

MIL: You . . . er . . . fixed all right for breakfast?

CHRIS (*looks across at* MAV): You heard the gentleman.

MAV: We've toast a . . . and tea.

CHRIS: What no eggs . . . no bacon?

MAV: They don't grow on trees.

MIL: Here . . . (*He hands* CHRIS *some loose change.*) use this up. I'll . . . I'll see you.

(MIL *goes out.* CHRIS *hands him the bucket and shuts the door.*)

CHRIS (*showing the cash*): He's a regular Daddy Christmas . . 'en he?

MINNIE: I wonder where he gets it from?

CHRIS: Got a doting Dad I expect.

MAV: His father's dead . . . he said so last night.

CHRIS: Mum then . . . I'm not fussy. I'll shop. (*False exit.*) I'll need a coat.

(CHRIS *goes off to the bedroom.*)

MINNIE: He didn't look happy to me.

MAV: Mil you mean?

MINNIE: He looked a bit peaked around the eyes. Any ciggies?

MAV (*handing over cig.*): Who'd look happy after sleeping on this?

MINNIE: It's all right. Bit small but——

(CHRIS *comes running from the bedroom with the coat. He exits quickly pulling it on.*)

RAY (*off*): Come back you bastard!

MINNIE (*taking no notice*): These are Yankees. (*Looks at cig.*)

MAV: Everything we've got's Yankees.

(RAY *comes running on in nightwear.*)

RAY: Where's the bugger—— (*Sees* CHRIS *is not in the room and runs out of the front door.*)

MINNIE: Can't look a gift horse I suppose.

(*There is a clatter off and a howl from* RAY.)

RAY: Oooh me bloody toe!

(*He comes limping on.*)

MINNIE: You're making a lot of noise this morning.

RAY: Who stuck that cow-handed bucket out there?

MAV: It's raining.

RAY: So what's the bloody roof for? Decoration?

MAV: You know there's a leak there. (*Returns to the kitchen.*)

RAY: We ought to complain to the landlord. He's liable to keep his premises fit for living in.

MINNIE: He's liable to want his rent too.

RAY: What we need is a quick load of lolly from somewhere.
(*Sitting and rubbing his toe.*)

MINNIE: Don't tell me you're feeling sorry for the landlord.

RAY: Bugger him! I mean to get a classy pad. . . . It'd be nice to have a bit of sex in splendour for a change.

MINNIE: Getting choosy in your old age.

RAY: You've got to admit it'd be nice to have a good springy bed . . . say a dunlopillo——

MINNIE: With one of them electric blankets under you——

RAY: And a mirror up above you.

MINNIE (*making a face*): Urgh . . . I wouldn't like that.

RAY: Course you would. Never say your mother bred a quitter!

MAV (*coming to beside him with a cup of tea*): There's something up between Bill and the American.

RAY: Something up? What sort of up? I'll have one of them. (*He grabs out as* MAV *takes a cig. from a packet.*)

MAV: I don't know where you learnt your manners.

RAY: Down the Bull Ring Saturday nights.

MINNIE: What's this about something up?

MAV: I think they've had a row.

RAY: Well, let's face it he had a flea in his ear after Bill gave him the glad—— (*Starts to look round.*)

MINNIE: Bill was a bit nasty there——

RAY: Ah, not nasty . . . it was just a lark . . . a bit of fun.

MINNIE: He was making out he was perverted.

RAY: He was just having a giggle.

MINNIE: I don't think it's funny.

RAY: He didn't do anything——

MINNIE: . . . Not whips and things——

RAY: . . . anything. And the Yank shot out like he was scalded.

MINNIE: I don't blame him.

RAY: Has anybody seen the bloody matches?

MAV: Use the fire.

(RAY *bends down over the electric fire and lights cigarette.*)

MINNIE: Didn't you think it was nasty? (*To* MAV.)

(*Pause.*)

Well did you?

MAV: I didn't think it was wise.

RAY: You didn't think it was what? (*Straightening up from fire.*)

MAV: I said I didn't think it was wise. He might not have come back.

RAY (*sarcastically*): I'd have been heart-broken.
  (JANET *enters.*)
  To say nothing of tootsie wee here.
JANET: You pulled every stitch of clothes off me.
RAY: It was Chris whipping the coat.
JANET: We ought to have another blanket.
MAV: Perhaps Milton will oblige if you ask him.
JANET: A right nit I'd look asking a feller to buy me a blanket!
MAV: If he was to move——
JANET: Who's got the fags?
MAV (*tossing the packet*): If he was to move in I bet you'd get them.
  (*Pause.*)
RAY: Move in here?
MAV: He's as good as in already. What's to stop us going the whole hog?
  (*Pause.*)
JANET: Who's got a light?
RAY: Use that. (*Points to the fire.*)
JANET: You do it. (*Hands him cigarette.*)
RAY: I'll wash your feet if you like.
JANET: I don't trust them things. Put your hand wrong and you've got a blue flash and a funeral.
MINNIE: It'd make the numbers odd.
MAV: I don't see that matters.
  (*Pause.*)
RAY: I'd like to hear what Bill'd have to say about that.
MAV: Bill's only one of us.
  (*Pause.*)
JANET: There's no saying he'd come.
MINNIE: He's not like us anyhow . . . look at last night.
MAV: He came back . . . he might have run out but he came back. That shows something.
RAY: What?
MAV: That he's lonely . . . that he wants friends.
MINNIE: Did it take you till last night to find that out?
MAV: All I mean is——
MINNIE: Why do you think he was sniffing round Janet?

JANET: I don't like the way you say that.
MAV: If you'll just listen——
RAY: I'd like to know where Bill's gone.
MAV: Never mind about him——
RAY: It looks a bit crummy to me, waking up with Yankee here and him gone.
MAV: I told you they looked as——
JANET: What's this about Bill then?
MAV: —as if they'd had a row.
MINNIE: He's not here.
JANET: Not here? Where is he?

(CHRIS *pushes open the door and enters with groceries.*)

CHRIS: Right . . . get cooking.

(*He dumps the food on the table.*)

JANET: You been at the telephone boxes again?
CHRIS: Don't be a cheeky chick . . . and I got news for you lot.
RAY: About Bill?
CHRIS: I dunno . . . but there's a plain-clothed cop hanging round the corner.

(RAY *goes to the window.*)

RAY: Get on!
JANET: If he's in plain clothes how——
CHRIS: His feet, lovey . . . and plain-clothed cops smell of moth balls.
MAV: It can't be anything to do with us.
MINNIE: It might be his doing the telephone box.
CHRIS: If he'd have wanted me he'd have took me.
RAY (*returning*): It's a cop all right.
CHRIS: I told you. I can smell them a mile off.
JANET: The moth balls you mean?
MINNIE: Maybe they've heard of the big job you're always planning.
MAV (*to* CHRIS): Or the pot you're carrying.

(*Pause.*)

RAY: Who's carrying pot?

(MAV *looks at* CHRIS. *All follow suit.*)

CHRIS (*laughs*): I'm all here you know . . . there's nothing missing.

JANET: You haven't got any pot, have you?
CHRIS: Why? You want some?
RAY (*to* MAV): How d'you know he got pot?
MAV: I was looking for a match, earlier on.
   (MINNIE *goes to the window and looks out.*)
CHRIS: That cop's not on to me.
RAY: How the hell can you know that? They're hot.
CHRIS: 'Cos I know what I'm doing.
RAY: Looks like they know too.
JANET: You want to get rid of it. If they find it here they——
MINNIE: Bill's coming——
RAY: How much you got?
CHRIS (*to* MAV): What about getting cooking?
JANET: You want to be sensible, Chris, a——
RAY: Never mind about cooking . . . if they come up here and find pot we're all in stook.
CHRIS (*laughs*): You got cold feet!
MINNIE: He's talking to Bill——
   (*They all go to the window except* MAV. *She sits smoking.*)
CHRIS: It's a right wet job he's got there.
JANET (*giggles*): It's a bit like James Bond, 'en it?
MINNIE: If he looks up here and sees us lot looking down——
RAY: Min's right . . . come on out of it——
   (RAY *starts to push everyone away from the window.*)
JANET: Give over——
CHRIS: What's the panic?
RAY: If you've got pot on you we'd better get rid of it.
CHRIS: You're in a state——
RAY: Pot smells . . . one whiff and they'll take the place apart.
CHRIS: There's nothing to worry about.
RAY: You don't know cops——
CHRIS (*to* MAV): Come on, Mav. I'm starving.
MAV: What have you got it for anyway?
CHRIS: Business, Mav . . . business . . . now how about cooking so——
MAV: I don't like that sort of business——
CHRIS: You like lolly though.
MAV: Not that way.

CHRIS: Suit yourself. (*He picks up food.*) I can cook too if I have to.
(*He goes towards the kitchen.*)
RAY (*coming in front of him*): Wait a minute.
CHRIS: To do a big job you need nerve. You don't have it. So let me get on with it.
MINNIE: What were you going to do with what you get for it?
CHRIS: I'm not just out to feather my own nest. (*He goes into the kitchen.*) I got loyalty.
RAY: The only nest you'll get us'll have bars on it ... and it won't be feathered, believe you me.
CHRIS: Don't get panicky. (*Preparing bacon and eggs on stove.*) I keep telling you ... there's no——
RAY: Where've you got it? Where is it?
CHRIS: Keep your nose out.
RAY: If you've got it here we——
CHRIS: —just leave it to Daddy.
RAY: Where've you got the bloody stuff? (*He grabs* CHRIS*'s arm.*)
CHRIS: Mind the egg.
RAY: I'm not playing.
CHRIS: Oh grow up. (*He jerks his arm free.*)
RAY: You little bugger! (*He grabs at* CHRIS.)
CHRIS: Get off—— (*He closes with* RAY.)

JANET ⎫
MINNIE ⎬ (*together*):
RAY ⎥
CHRIS ⎭

Oh gawd——
Take it easy——
I'll fix you——
Mind your bloody hands——

JANET ⎫ (*together*):
MINNIE ⎭

Stop it, Ray——
Leave him, Chris——

(RAY *and* CHRIS *struggle and stagger, falling on the settee. The door opens and* BILL *comes in. He is soaked from the rain.*)
BILL: Is it sexual?
RAY (*getting up*): He's trading in pot!
BILL: Don't tell me you were striking a moral blow. (*Takes off his jacket.*)
CHRIS (*rubbing his lip*): You've cut my lip, you stupid cow.
MAV (*tossing towel to* BILL): Here.

RAY: He'll have us all in clink.
CHRIS: Tell him to shut up.
BILL: You sort yourself out.
CHRIS: He's all brute force and bloody ignorance.
    (RAY *takes a step forward.*)
MINNIE: Cut it out, Ray. It doesn't help any. (*Stopping him.*)
BILL: Quite right. If you must fight bugger off somewhere else and indulge.
MAV: Is that all you've got to say?
BILL: U Thant gets paid money for doing less.
JANET: What about the copper down there?
BILL: Working I suppose.
RAY: Oh very funny. We thought he was selling dirty postcards.
BILL: Well you're out of luck. Funny job . . . still it's a living. It's a way to earn a crust. (*To* MAV.) What's for breakfast?
MAV: If you want it, cook it yourself.
BILL: Oh, got a touch of the Lysystratas have we?
MAV: I'd like something to be taken seriously for a change.
BILL: I am serious. I'm starving. (*To* CHRIS.) You eaten?
CHRIS: I was just getting frying when——
BILL: You mean she's not just picking on me?
RAY: She's worried about that cop down there and so am I.
BILL: Perhaps they've discovered you've a big job in mind.
RAY: And we've every right to be while he's got pot here.
BILL: My bet is that that cop's there because the powers that be think we're running a knocking shop. Or a disorderly house, or a bawdy house. I understand there is some moot difference in law. (*Starts to take off shoes and dry feet.*)
MINNIE: Well of all the nerve!
BILL: It is a bit cheeky, isn't it? (*To* MAV.) Now what about the essen?
RAY: How do you know what they think?
    (MINNIE *goes to the window.*)
BILL: I said to him—looking at his feet—I said to him, "Excuse me, officer, but I'm thinking of joining the force, could you give me a few tips." I think it upset him.
MINNIE: I can't see him.
BILL: There, see? He's gone. But he will be back soon, never

fear. With a recruiting sergeant! What happened to Yankee Doodle Dandyo?

MAV: Did you have a row with him last night?

BILL: That's a good question. It's got a nuance to it. A let's look at the facts nuance. You are afraid he's bolted off and removed our sole means of support?

MAV: It's a change for you to think about how we manage to keep going.

BILL: There is no matrimony here—no one need stay who can feed better elsewhere.

MAV: Matrimony or not when I'm given a promise I expect it to be kept. Especially when it's wrapped up in a lot of nonconformist idealism.

BILL: Another bit of my nonconformist idealism is—consider the lilies of the field, they toil not neither do they spin——

MAV: If Chris's anything to go on they become robbers, pot peddlers and ponces instead.

BILL: And that concludes our grace before meals, children. We may now get our noses into the trough.

(BILL *opens a packet of cereal and begins to pour it into a dish.*)

MAV: Bill, what's got into you?

BILL: I'm wondering what the female of ponce is.

(MAV *turns and goes out of the room. Pause.* BILL *pours milk and sugar on his cereal.*)

(*eats*) I like the added viamin—it may not aid one's potency but it does make them taste less foul.

MINNIE: You've come back in a right old mood, haven't you?

BILL: Mav still lives in a sort of Rupert Brookian nightmare, that doesn't agree with me. I wish I'd won you last night, Minnie my old lay by.

CHRIS: You didn't sleep with Mav last night.

BILL (*eyeing him over the spoon*): Did I say I did?

CHRIS: It sounds like what you meant.

BILL: Well fancy that! It sounds like what I meant!

CHRIS (*to others*): Didn't that sound like what he meant?

JANET: Don't ask me.

BILL: Let us review ourselves . . . let us try to sound like what we all meant.

MINNIE: I wish you'd pack it in!

BILL: Suicide is too logical for this illogical world.

MINNIE: Oh Gawd! Make some tea, Chris . . . he's on one of his jags.

CHRIS: Maybe Mav's pregnant!

(*They all look at him.*)

She's sick in the mornings.

(*He goes into the kitchen and puts the kettle on. Pause.*)

BILL: It will be no wise child if she is.

MINNIE: That's not very nice.

BILL: What is there nice about the idea to be nice about?

MINNIE: It's nothing to make jokes about anyway.

BILL: All the more reason for looking on the funny side. (*He lifts his spoon.*) Should I go easy on the milk? Mav might need it.

MINNIE: I'll fetch you one—sure as heaven I will.

BILL: That'd be turning a comedy into a farce.

JANET: If it was you having it you wouldn't be laughing.

BILL: True . . . but everybody else would be. I daresay even the Osservator Romana would be hard put to restrain a giggle.

RAY: Why don't you get stuffed!

(*Pause.*)

BILL: If you can keep your head when all about you are losing theirs and blaming it on you——

(BILL *spoons the cereal.* RAY *knocks it from his hand. Pause.* BILL *picks up the spoon.*)

See what I mean?

RAY: If Mav's pregnant it means she might have a baby.

BILL (*laughs*): Give him his due. He knows the facts of life.

RAY: It's not a bloody joke.

BILL: *Min*'s already pointed that out.

RAY: Something's got to be done.

BILL: *Mav*'s pointed that out. Your reply was "Do a big job". Well, you do one. Get into the Bank of England and keep her and her young in luxury.

CHRIS: He hasn't enough nerve to get into a meat safe.

RAY: You won't learn, will you—— (*Moving in.*)
MINNIE (*stopping him*): We've had enough of that.
BILL: And enough is as good as a feast they say! Where's the tea?
JANET: Do you think I ought to take Mav a cup?
   (CHRIS *collects pot etc., from the kitchen.*)
MINNIE: I should leave her a bit.
JANET: I just wanted to do something.
BILL: Cook two eggs, two rashers of bacon and fry a slice of bread.
MINNIE: What about Mav? You've got to think of her.
BILL: Am I supposed to give up eating in sympathy or something?
MINNIE: There's the future to consider.
BILL: And I help by starving now?
JANET: That's you all over. Eat everything today and leave nothing for tomorrow.
BILL: Is she that far gone?
JANET: You know what I mean.
RAY: He can't take anything seriously. Never could.
BILL (*to* CHRIS, *taking tea*): You got any comments on my character?
CHRIS: I didn't know you had one.
BILL (*looks round*): I have the feeling the meeting is against me.
MINNIE: Becoming a mother——
JANET: Having a baby——
   (*Both stop.*)
   Go on——
MINNIE: No you——
JANET: I was just saying that having a baby is . . . well . . . it's——
MINNIE: —a serious business——
JANET: Exactly. Very serious.
MINNIE: Something to think about.
JANET: It's sacred really.
RAY: Holy.
MINNIE: It's a new life.
JANET: Needing warmth.

RAY: Comfort.
MINNIE: A home——
RAY: Security.
JANET: Tenderness.
MINNIE: Love.
BILL: Urrrr. (*He makes a sound like a regurgitation of disgust.*)
(*They all look at him.*)
Something important has happened in England again . . . unto us a child is given . . . and of course, naturally our first question must be—will this help the stability of the pound? Will it get sterling into a fine old nick again? Set our people free? And echo answers what? Not bloody likely! It will increase the consumer market—a cardinal sin against the new morality. Hand back your Queen's award for industry.
RAY: I'm beginning to dislike you.
CHRIS: You don't seem to have a heart.
BILL: Perhaps it's the wrong kind. I'll fly to the Cape and get a black one. (*Sips tea.*) You make a rotten cup of tea!
(*He gets up.* RAY *and* CHRIS *move in front of him. He sits.*)
My case rests. (*Pause.*) What happens now?
RAY: You tell us.
BILL: That is a question . . . a good question.
MINNIE: We need money.
JANET: Mav'll need looking after.
CHRIS: I'm willing to do something for the good of us all.
RAY: I've always been willing to do a job.
MINNIE: I don't like either way.
JANET: But they have been willing.
MINNIE: Oh yes. They've been willing.
RAY (*to* BILL): What about you?
BILL: The Good Lord will provide . . . and if he lets us down the State'll step in.
RAY: Or maybe you could step out.
(*Pause.* BILL *looks at them.*)
BILL: This is my flat . . . I brought you here. Remember?
CHRIS: That makes you responsible for what's happened then, doesn't it?

BILL: I feel that is putting the argument at too high a philosophical level.

JANET: It is your fault. What happened to Mav could've happened to any of us.

BILL (*with a glance at* JANET): Who's got the coffin nails?

MINNIE (*supplying them*): They're only Americans.

BILL: I didn't bring him here.

RAY: He's done nothing wrong. There's no harm in him.

JANET: He's helped us a lot.

MINNIE: I like him.

CHRIS (*pointedly*): Mav likes him too.

BILL (*he takes a long breath*): I don't have to be a genius to see how the wind bloweth, do I? Here is the weather forecast—bloody unbelievable!

MINNIE: You've got to see Bill that——

BILL: I can see . . . I can see very clearly that this is not a problem that is going to be solved by a ruthless clamp down on hire purchase! Nor by the votes of delegates in Congress assembled. It is the bull of the herd, the tiger on the hill, the cock robin on his cabbage patch who's stuck with working this out.

CHRIS: He's bloody nuts!

(*The door opens and* MILTON *comes in*. BILL *turns to him*.)

BILL: Well! A right doxological Donnybrook you've just missed, my doxy! They love you. Their hearts are panting for your cooling stream of dollars! (*Goes to* BILL.) Let the Viets save themselves, there's a great society here with a dose of the Brummagem glowers. Save that. (*Pushes* MILTON *towards the others*.)

MIL: Where did you get to?

BILL: Nature has demonstrated what we had overlooked. Sex is not simply an entertainment for a tired society. Sex is functional—and has functioned on Mav with considerable efficiency. She's pregnant.

MIL: I don't see why you should be surprised.

BILL: Isn't he a practical man? Right down to fundamentals . . . no messing about. The straight censure in the fatherly voice. It is because he loves us all that we fear his wrath!

CHRIS: Do you mind if we have our say?
BILL: Remember. Americans write the best British histories—it doesn't follow you should hand them your future.
RAY: Gab up.
BILL: I am simply—

RAY ⎫
CHRIS ⎪ (*together*):
MINNIE ⎬
JANET ⎭

I said gab up.
Will you shut up!
Keep quiet for a bit.
Pack it in, Bill.

(*Pause.*)

BILL: Well, I've had a happy life. I may as well eat. (*Goes into kitchen.*)
JANET: Come and sit down, Milton.
RAY: Yeah . . . take a seat, Mil. (*Holds out chair.*)
MIL (*looking into kitchen*): Is he all right?
MINNIE: He's a glutton for grub.
RAY: Not only for grub either.
CHRIS: Go on . . . make yourself at home.

(MIL *looks across at the kitchen.* BILL *waves. He is cooking.*)

BILL (*dramatically*): Repent not! Do not blush to tell,
               If need be to their faces,
               How you and I went down to hell
               Escorted by the Graces.

(*They all sit.* BILL *goes on with his frying.*)

RAY: We'd like you to know that we appreciate what you've done for us. (*To the others.*) Isn't that right?
JANET: He's been very kind.
MINNIE (*confidentially*): We've always thought he (*Nods to kitchen.*) was a bit round the bend.
MIL: Have you?
RAY: Well, haven't you?
MIL: No, not really. I've always rather liked him.
RAY: Ah, now we're not saying we dislike him . . . he's all right in his way. (*To others.*) Isn't he?
MINNIE: If you happen to like his way.
RAY: Now easy, Min——
MINNIE: I'm only being honest. I used to quite like him . . . but not since he's been so heartless about Mav.

RAY: That's it . . . he has been heartless.
JANET: I didn't like his attitude, I must say.
CHRIS: There's no point in beating about the bush. He's turned sour to us. We don't want him here. We'll never make anything with him. He's not interested——
RAY: It's true. He's not. We've all had ideas for making a packet but he's just laughed at them.
MINNIE: I used to think he could fix things——
JANET: But he can't, let's face it.
CHRIS: So what about moving in here with us?
(*Pause.* MIL *looks to the kitchen.*)
BILL (*calls*): We must sacrifice something for England! Our productivity is up. Our price must be kept down. In future we shall copulate six full nights a week! (*Bangs the pan.*) On the seventh only shall we rest and renew our strength.
CHRIS: I tell you he's nuts.
MINNIE: What's he mean about keeping our price down?
JANET: Cheek. We've never had a penny off him.
BILL: Communards unite! We have nothing to lose but our chromosone counts! (*He peels a rasher and holds it over the pan.*) Oh pig, forgive me! You look good, you'll taste good— (*He turns to the others.*) But it's still bloody murder, 'en it? (*Turns back to the pan.*)
CHRIS (*to* MIL): Well, what do you say?
MIL: I don't approve of dishonesty—stealing.
BILL (*singing*): The Lord high Bishop Orthodox—the vagabond in the stocks . . . they all shall equal be!
RAY: Nobody'd ask you to do anything.
MIL: If I live in a community I'm responsible—at least I have some responsibility—for how that community lives. For its ethics.
CHRIS: We'd do what you say. (*To others.*) Wouldn't we?
(BILL *comes from the kitchen with plate of cooked food and bread etc. He pushes between* RAY *and* MINNIE.)
BILL: C'mon, I still have some rights. It's my table.
RAY: Not for long it's not——
BILL (*about* MIL): He's an honest man—aren't you, my old cocker? He covets not his brother's ox nor his ass, nor his

maid servant, nor anything that is his . . . or to be more
precise he covets but will not take . . . only buy. A fine
distinction with an indistinct difference.
CHRIS: If you must talk, talk sense.
MIL: All I want to do is help—in any way I can.
BILL: You know my creed. We pass this way but once—so
anyone we can kick in the balls as we're passing let us so
do.
JANET: That's a nice thing to say!
BILL: You can't be nice . . . (*Takes a mouthful.*) . . . defending
your own.
MINNIE: You are a glutton.
BILL: But not greedy . . . I never kept a florin to myself, did I,
brother Ray?
RAY: That florin is a personal heirloom.
BILL: So was my privacy . . . and his dope. (*To* MIL.) You'll
have to learn. Buy one and you buy all . . . only the
animal's instinctive. Everything else is a moral act. A
key—your own commercial break. (*Indicating* MINNIE.) At
six she was a butterfly in Noddyland and her drawers
dropped down. She's never managed to get them up again.
(*Indicating* JANET.) Symbol of the age—a margarine girl
and ninety-nine men out of a hundred can't tell her from
butter.
JANET (*to* MIL): Should I slap his face?
RAY (*to* MIL): I said he was nuts, didn't I?
MINNIE (*to* MIL): And I'd like you to know that I pulled them
up quick! It was the elastic.
CHRIS (*to* MIL): Never mind about him . . . are you coming in
with us?
MIL: What will . . . will he be staying?
CHRIS: We'll fix him.
RAY: Don't worry—we will.
   (*Pause.*)
BILL (*in Americanese*): Now's your chance. Give me your tired,
your hungry, your poor, your teeming masses, longing to
be free. Send me your tempest tossed, the wretched refuse
of your stricken shore. Give me these—provided they are

white anglo-saxon protestant with adequate means of support.

MIL: None of us is perfect, Bill, we can only try—and I won't turn my back on them.

BILL: As there is no God, men must become Gods . . . but not necessarily tribal ones. (*He eats.*) I have cooked this pig to perfection.

MIL: What about the child . . . what will . . . what can you do about that?

BILL: That's Mav's affair.

MINNIE: Trust a man to say that.

BILL: This needs a bit more sauce.

CHRIS (*to* RAY): Shall we chuck him out?

RAY: He's asked for it.

(CHRIS *and* RAY *rise.*)

MIL: No, wait—— (*He gets in front of them.*)

BILL: He's my friend too, you see.

MIL: We can sort this out without—— (*Touches* BILL.)

BILL: I still think it needs more sauce.

(*He reaches for the sauce but* MINNIE *and* JANET *grab it.*)
I thought you only took tomato.
(*Pause.*)
I tell you what. Ask Mav. If she wants me to go, I'll do the honest thing.

RAY: She can't get rid of you quick enough.

BILL: I have confidence in my charm. Go on . . . ask her.

MINNIE: I'll do it. (*Goes off.*)

BILL (*facing them all across the table*): By the way . . . a little news. If I do leave it will be voluntarily. I've paid the rent . . . oh yes . . . I'm a tenant in good standing now.

CHRIS: Where did you get the lolly?

BILL: I have my talents . . . ways and means . . . tea anyone?

RAY: I don't believe you!

BILL: You can always ask the landlord . . . this is my castle . . . legally. I may surrender but it won't be taken from me.
(*Lifts his cup.*) To England, home and camaraderie.
(MINNIE *comes in.*)

MINNIE: She's gone! She's walked out . . . left us.

JANET: What, Mav has?
MINNIE: Her case has gone . . . she's packed her things and gone.
RAY: She'd never——
MINNIE: She has I tell you.
RAY: How could she have gone . . . she's got no way out.
JANET: She'd have to come through here, wouldn't she?
RAY: Course she would——
  (*He goes out.*)
BILL: Now we'll get some news . . . Sherlock Holmes is on the job.
CHRIS: Perhaps he'll disappear too.
  (RAY *reappears.*)
  (*To* MIN.) My luck's out, see.
RAY: It's a bloody mystery.
MINNIE: She could have crept across.
BILL: Like the cat in the crypt, you mean?
MIN: We ought to tell the police.
RAY: You barmy!
JANET: He upset her. You never know what she might have done.
CHRIS: Never mind what she's done . . . what the bloody hell do we do?
  (*Pause.*)
BILL: I tell you what. Move in with him. (*Nods at* MIL.)
  (MINNIE, JANET, RAY *and* CHRIS *look at* MIL.)
MIL (*looks at* BILL): O.K. . . . get your things.
  (JANET, MINNIE, RAY *and* CHRIS *go off to the bedroom. Pause.*)
  I'm sorry it had to end like this.
BILL (*takes a wallet from his pocket. Hands it to* MIL): I took my wages.
MIL (*puts his hand to his pocket*): I hadn't missed it. (*Puts wallet in pocket.*) Look, Bill . . . I'm sorry it had to end like this—— (*Takes* BILL's *arm.*)
  (BILL *with a sudden gesture of rage throws* MIL *across the room.* MIL *falls against a chair. He stays there.* BILL *looks down on him then goes and picks up his modelling clay.*)
BILL: I shall model a Pelagian whore!
MIL (*up*): We can't change ourselves, Bill.

BILL: No—we don't have to betray ourselves either.
  (MINNIE, JANET, RAY *and* CHRIS *enter with bundles.*)
MIL (*to them*): You've only taken your own stuff?
BILL: Everything I have's in there. (*Points to box.*) It was a precaution.
  (MINNIE, JANET, RAY *and* CHRIS *stand in line by the door.*)
CHRIS: C'mon, Mil.
  (*They go out.*)
BILL (*To* MIL.): Your penance——
  (MIL *puts his hand to his pocket, takes out wallet.*)
  No thank you. I've mine to come.
  (MIL *shrugs, puts the wallet back in his pocket.* BILL *models.* MIL *goes out. As the door shuts* BILL *goes over to the window. Looks out, watches. Turns back into the room. Goes to the table and clears it. Takes a key from his pocket, opens box. Takes out a clean cloth and napkins and cups etc. Lays table. In the centre a vase of plastic flowers. He dusts these wryly and with some disgust goes to kitchen and starts to wash up.*)
  (MAV *enters.* BILL *turns.*)
MAV (*giving* BILL *a key*): It's dusty in that cupboard.
BILL (*taking key*): We'll have a clean out. Do the place up.
  (BILL *goes into the kitchen. Starts to cook a meal.* MAV *arranges the table.*)
MAV: I'd like that.
BILL: Good.
  (*Pause.*)
MAV: Nice to be on our own again.
BILL: Lovely.
  (MAV *sits and undoes her napkin.*)
  But as Lucretius says—
  (MAV *turns.*)
  It's all holes.
  (*He cooks.* MAV *arranges her napkin.*)

THE END